£1-50 4/9?

D0539623

—The
LAST
SUMMER

The — LAST SUMMER

IAIN CRICHTON SMITH

RICHARD DREW PUBLISHING

Glasgow

First published 1969
by Victor Gollancz Ltd.

This edition first published 1986
by RICHARD DREW PUBLISHING LIMITED
6 Clairmont Gardens, Glasgow G3 7LW
Scotland

Reprinted 1989

The publisher acknowledges the financial assistance
of the Scottish Arts Council in the publication of this book.

Copyright © 1969 Iain Crichton Smith

The verses by W. H. Auden, quoted on pages 36, 40 and 111-13
are from "A Bride in the Thirties" and are reprinted from *Some
Poems, 1940* by kind permission of the Author and the
publishers, Faber & Faber.
The text of the Authorised Version of the Bible is Crown
copyright and the extracts used herein are reproduced
by permission.

British Library Cataloguing in Publication Data

Smith, Iain Crichton
    The last summer.–(Scottish collection)
    I. Title   II. Series
    823'.914[F]   PR6005.R58

    ISBN 0-86267-163-9
    ISBN 0-86267-162-0 Pbk

Printed in Great Britain by
Cox & Wyman Ltd, Reading

HE WAS SITTING on the peat bank looking south. It was a fine day and the moor, spongy under his feet, was covered with heather bells: a breeze gently stirred his trousers. The sky above him was a blue inverted vase, unflawed, unscarred; and in the depths of it a skylark was singing deliriously. He had a book in his hand which he wasn't reading. He was sixteen years old and it was wartime. Somewhere else guns were being fired, sailors were being drowned. Here there was no sound; no sound whatsoever except for the humming of a bee or the skylark, or the buzz of a fly. Below him, the peats were set in their black pyramids, wet, dripping and new. The peat bank itself was a shiny scar among other shiny scars on the moor. He swung his legs down over the edge of the peat bank and looked down, conscious of his body. The pages of his book fluttered in the slight breeze. He looked south.

It was there she lived. He had never seen the house for it was in a different village from his own, about three miles away across the moor. He could walk there in the direction of the sea and look at it, the house where she stayed, the house where she woke at morning and slept at night. His thoughts about her were pure. She was a goddess, someone out of a Greek or Roman book of legends. She walked on air. She was clothed with fire, as the poets wrote. She was so far above him that he could not aspire to her. She was sixteen years old and lived in that village three miles away and he had never seen her house. But sometimes he would come out to the moor by himself and look south, to where she lived, dreaming of her. It was impossible to do other than dream about her.

What else could he do? What chance would he ever have of doing anything else? He was a worm. He was a good scholar. He played football rather well. But he couldn't swim and he wasn't a fighter. He ticked off all the things he couldn't do. He knew nothing about mechanical things: he couldn't do algebra well, though he was good at geometry. In some things he was slow: in other things he was very quick. But the trouble was that what he was quick at, other than football, were scholarly things, like Latin or English or geometry. He hated having to climb the roof to put the felt on it. He didn't like tarring the roof or mending fences. He was clumsy. There was no way round it. He was not suited to her. Furthermore, he was poor and he had no style. He was liable to blush, he couldn't talk to a girl. In fact, he was useless.

For instance, there was Ronny: he knew everything about girls. He was as much at ease with them as he was with boys, perhaps more so. He hated Ronny, envying him his grace, his sophisticated manners, his air of rich negligence. He envied him his deceptively lazy mind, his almost adult self-possession, his cleverness among people, and that subtle, dangerous quality in him which could turn almost to sadism. Why, he had even taken her to the cinema a few times. He had told everyone about it. Oh, God, imagine him with her in the cinema in the darkness. Malcolm's mind spawned images of light and dark, chocolates and oranges, white limbs and red plush seats, coquettish glances in the night of the folk.

Oh, God, he couldn't bear it. In this summer, this last summer which ought to be perfect and unflawed like the sky but wasn't and never would be again. He banged his hand down savagely on the book. These wasted years of learning, had they not left him clumsy and terrified? Staring south he thought of her, black-haired, the blood coursing vigorously under the skin of her face which had the sheen of a rare fruit, a redness which was not raw but like a fruit, delicate. Of course there were so many rednesses. The redness of blood, the redness of carrots, the redness of beetroot, the redness of plush seats. None of these was her redness. He thought of a Gaelic proverb about the highest apple on the bough, and was uncomforted again because it told of her infinite distance. She, in her schoolgirl's uniform, with her smile, her white teeth. The swell of her, under the navy blue. The yellow belt at her waist. Her voice. The slanted look in her eyes as if she were eternally laughing, bubbling over. And looking south she was there by the sea. At this moment she was there. What was she doing now? Only to be with her would be enough. To be her dog. To look at her, to breathe in her vicinity. Not even to speak if that did not suit her.

And if she had even asked him for a Latin book. If she had asked him to translate Cicero or Vergil for her. But she didn't care. She wasn't interested in scholarship. Or perhaps others were teaching, construing for her. Perhaps even in that village hundreds of miles away there was a pet tutor sweating over her Euclid and her Vergil, content to do this if nothing else for her, a slave to her Roman grace. Nor did she ever ask him to explain the theorems, and yet the class was not a large one, taught by that idiotic football-managing bald-headed Warhorse. Perhaps she hadn't even noticed him, not really noticed him, the him below the one she saw. And yet he was in love with her and would be till he died. No matter how old he was he would remember her. She would be his desperate love. In the south. Where the breeze played over the heather bells. Where the moor was blood red.

"I would even fight for her," he thought. Imagine it. Suppose the Germans landed there, he would defend her with stones, with forks, with knives. If he were only given a gun he would hold the house against thousands of them in their silvery uniforms. In fact he would even fight the Japs for her. He thought of himself climbing into a plane, pulling back the joystick, waving down at her from his serious goggled face, turning south, zigzagging, determined to return to her but to die if that was necessary. He would stand on beaches—the last to leave—throwing grenades; he would stand on the last deck on the last ship, pumping shells into a hot gun; he would be tied to the stake for her while the Germans or the Japs in their fierce gutturals complimented him on his courage, dragging his guts out. But, try as he might, when he looked up into the sky he saw only Ronny in the pilot's seat, with his negligent, devil-may-care expression. And there she was in the south, with her navy blue pinafore belted with yellow, unconcerned about Cicero.

He picked up the book with a sigh and turned home, kicking the turf as he went along, slamming stones away from him with a vicious swearing curve, climbing the moorland, startling a lark from its nest and glancing for a moment with tender care at the warm, sunny, speckled eggs. He had never seen a plover's egg nor an eagle's. What would an eagle's egg be like? Lark's eggs were common. You found the nests near cart tracks, the eggs tanned and speckled. He remembered when he was younger running about in his shorts, taking the peats home in a wheel-barrow. How long ago that seemed! Running barefoot to school while the headmaster waited with the whistle in his mouth and you ran like the wind and the iron bell clanged and the strawberries were growing in the garden and the teachers—all women—were waiting to welcome you into their huge arms and bosoms and the walls were bright with all the maps of the world.

More serious now, and older, he headed home.

[2]

THERE WERE ABOUT sixty houses in the village, ringed on one side by the moor and on the other by the sea, with a river not too far distant. In winter the wind swept across the bare level, lashing at houses and fences, lifting the hens and driving them helter skelter to their deaths where the crows hovered. In winter too there was rain blurring the sea where the boats bobbed on the slate-grey water.

Sometimes he would sit dreamily by the window watching the rain pouring down the panes and the sea's restless leaping white horses, like hounds in at a final hunt, baying an invisible prey. In winter, the wind howled in the wide chimney, the grass swayed all yellow, uncombing itself, the ditches ran with wild water, and the blackbirds were cuffed down the sky by a terrible slapping hand. The clouds raced overhead and lightning flashed and thunder ran, one-footed in the ditch. The sheep cowered by walls in their used wool, horses shook in the cold, their fine skins streaming with rain. The roads were rutted and slippery. The bewildering snow made a manic pattern on the earth and in the air.

In summer it was different. To wake on a summer morning was bliss. To walk among the flowers; sometimes he used to try and walk so carefully that he wouldn't crush the daisies and the daffodils and the bluebells hiccuping up the slope. The air was full of perfume. Sometimes, taking the water home in buckets, he would lie on the earth listening to the humming of the bees, watching the red flowers growing among the potatoes. Springs of water gushed and bubbled and sparkled in clear air. There was the smell of tar from the road which was being mended. There was football to be played till late at night while the moon shone overhead, clear and bright as a ghostly football between invisible goalposts. In the hot summer days cows lashed their tails at the flies, and often he had watched them struck dumb in the heat, their eyes full of tears and flies, exhausted by the venom of summer.

Norman would be singing his songs early in the morning like the lark, but he was away now in the Navy. Perhaps he was singing there. Sometimes Malcolm and his brother Colin would be up in the attic swinging on the beams, leafing through old books which had been there for years, or boxing and hitting each other in that obscure struggle for supremacy that went on under the semblance of play. Sometimes he hated Colin. He seemed so unaware, so careless, so brutal, living purely by the senses while he himself was a dreamer. His brother was thirteen years old, three years younger than himself. He was afraid of nothing. He would climb the highest cliffs in search of seagull's nests. He was often out on a local boat in search of fish and arrived home with saithe for his mother, who would be waiting up for him till midnight. Nothing she said to him made the slightest difference. He obeyed none but himself. Strange how though he himself observed the rules his brother was preferred and admired more. At least he thought that this was true.

Saturday afternoon. Where was his brother now? Perhaps fishing for trout in a brook, perhaps building a tent with Dell, perhaps hunting rats. Once a rat had leaped straight at his throat and he had killed it with a stone as it catapulted straight through the air. Malcolm made his way down to the house. From the brow of the hill he could see it clearly with the thin blue smoke rising from the chimney, blown a little by the wind. He could see the washing on the line. No one could be seen except for Tinker mending a fence, raising a hammer with slow weighty dignity. The village was being emptied of its youth as the war continued. That evening he would spend translating Vergil. His mother would want him to be working. "To get on in the world", whatever that meant. She had worked hard bringing up the two boys ever since his father had died, so long ago that he couldn't remember him except that there was a picture of him on the sideboard, a small dapper alert man with a very live looking moustache and thin lips.

He kicked another stone ahead of him. He wished he could be out with the other boys, wherever they were. He never seemed to know where they were since he had left the local school and gone to the town one. Sometimes on Sundays they would be doing a little gambling, throwing pennies at sticks, but he had few pennies. His brother was still in school but would be leaving this year. He might become a fisherman. He certainly didn't like school and Malcolm thought that he himself was despised for staying.

The corn was growing well, the sea was calm today, the air clear and the sky blue. Why therefore was he so restless? More and more now he felt restless. Sometimes he would go away by himself for long periods into the solitude of the moor and sit there reading a book. Dreaming of ships with white sails, of countries full of tropical plants, of islands and of cities, of girls with brilliant stockings and brilliant smiles. The river sparkled along among the stones. Sometimes you could find very small trout there. His mother would be waiting in the house, cooking perhaps, making flat floury scones, preparing herring for their food, salt herring to go with the potatoes. They were poor but there was always enough food. There were always eggs from the hens, potatoes from the ground, herring from the sea, and sometimes they might get a present of fish.

At night, the Tilley lamp, brighter than electric, stood in the middle of the oilclothed table, casting its round circle of dazzling light. His mother would be sitting on the low green painted stool, knitting, darning, sewing. Always busy. Always hoping that he would do well. And this year was his last one in school. If he was lucky he might get to university. If he got a bursary things would be even better. At night the stars sparkled above the village, immensely vivid and animated with their intense voltage, a sieve in the sky. He could stretch out his hands to them. On the moor he could hear an owl hooting or see it sitting there in moonlight like a grandmother with spectacles. How clear and cool the night was. He liked the night best of all.

His brother and his sister were in the house. They were going to kill a cock.

[3]

THE COCK WAS inside the cage of the creel, upturned on the linoleumed floor, its beady eyes winking. Now and then it would turn its head and look down at the floor, then it would raise it and look up stonily. Its body was partly yellow, its comb red and serrated. It was quite old. When it looked down at the floor, it seemed to think that there ought to be something there which it might peck and eat.

"Where have you been?" said his mother. "I was going to send you to the shop."

"What did you want?" he said, looking at the cock which had begun to withdraw into itself, staring down at the floor without moving, its head on one side as if it were thinking, as if it knew that it was going to die.

"We need a mantle for the Tilley," said his mother.

His brother Colin was bending down, polishing the toes of a pair of bright black boots. He looked up and smiled suddenly, showing small white perfect teeth. His smile was always disarming.

"I suppose," he said, glancing at the cock, "we'd better get it over with if I'm going to the dance."

Malcolm looked at the cock with hatred. "If only I could kill you," he thought. And he wanted suddenly to pull the creel away, to hold its thin neck in his hands, the throat through which it crowed in the morning to announce the dawn, and squeeze the life out of it, to watch it die in its red and yellow splendour, in its colour and flame. But then he thought of Janet and was weakened again.

"Malcolm won't be going to any dance," said his mother to Colin. "He has his bursary to sit."

It amazed him how she knew about these things. All his life he would never speak to her about the school or exams or teachers, or bring home any gossip.

Sometimes she would say to him: "I heard that one of your teachers collapsed today, but you never thought of telling me. I had to hear it from Mrs Mackenzie and she has no son in that school. I felt so ashamed."

He didn't say anything this time either. Still, he knew that come evening he would be sitting there doing his Latin and his geometry.

"Are you going to the dance then?" he said to Colin.

"Yes, all the boys are going." He didn't ask Malcolm to come. He often boasted to the boys about how clever Malcolm was, though he would never say anything flattering to his face. Putting a blue handkerchief carefully in the breast pocket of his jacket that was lying on the back of a chair, he said suddenly to Malcolm, with a wicked grin:

"Would you like to kill the cock yourself?" Malcolm didn't answer. The cock was now crumpled into itself, huddled up like an old woman.

"Ah, well," said Colin, straightening slowly and walking across the green linoleum floor, his arms bare. He walked over to the creel, looking down at it for a moment. Then he knelt, squatting on his heels, looking in through the bars of the creel and poking his finger between them. The cock turned its head away.

Malcolm said: "What do we need to kill him for anyway? Can't we have herring?"

His mother, who was pouring hot water into a white basin with a blue line running across the top, said:

"You know very well that we always have meat on a Sunday." Suddenly Colin upended the creel. There was frantic fluttering of feathers, a swirling and flapping of wings all yellow and red, the snakelike neck thrusting this way and that in a storm of motion. Malcolm forced himself to look. Colin had seized the neck and was twisting it slowly in his hands, the veins standing out on his arms, his body rocking with the effort, his face as red as the cock's comb. Slowly the effort eased, the eyes of the cock glazed, the neck seemed to relax, colour seemed to go out of the body and Colin was standing up.

"There you are, mother." There was blood on his hands, dark red blood. His mother took the cock and began to pluck the feathers, first laying it on a piece of newspaper on the floor. From where he was standing Malcolm tried to read the headline. It said: "RAF hits Germany again."

Colin washed his hands carefully in the basin of hot water, soaping them lavishly, though soap was scarce. When he had finished he went outside and threw the bloodstained water into the grass, watching it for a moment as it soaked in. Then he filled the basin once more, this time with cold water, and washed his face and neck. Malcolm watched the back of his neck, the head inverted over the bowl.

"Did you hear how Dicky is today?" he asked. There was a gurgle from the basin.

"No," said Colin, "I didn't hear."

"Did you go and see him?"

"No."

Colin towelled himself with great force and then removed his dungarees and put on his creased navy blue trousers.

He said: "I wish I could play the melodeon. I really wish I could play the melodeon."

His mother snorted: "What next?"

Already he had tried to learn the Jew's harp but he wasn't very successful.

"I wish I could play it, just the same," said Colin, one leg inside the trousers, the other outside, and leaning against the mantelpiece for support.

"Who's playing it tonight?" said Malcolm, trying to read more of what the RAF had been doing in Germany.

"Big Dan, I suppose." Big Dan was exempt from war service because of his limp.

Malcolm was listening to the sound of the sea, which he could hear quite distinctly. He put on the kettle without being asked and set the table. Colin was by now standing in front of the mirror, putting on his blue jersey which his mother had knitted. He was bending, looking at himself in the mirror with great satisfaction and concentration. Then he began to comb his gingery hair, very carefully, finally smoothing it back with his hands.

"Know what I was doing this afternoon?" he asked suddenly.

"No," said Malcolm, taking saucers and cups out of the press.

"Collecting scrap. Me and Dell. We found an old tin roof and a hammer without a handle and two pails. And we went in to old Maggie and asked her for scrap. And we got an old fender. For the war effort, you know."

"I'd have gone with you if you'd told me," said Malcolm, leaning over to read the paper.

Colin said : "I forgot. Anyway, you've got your work to do."

Malcolm suddenly felt a wave of affection for his brother. He thought : "I'll be in university and he'll be out on a ship on the sea, or if the worst comes to the worst he'll be working in a mill. And he doesn't envy me or anything. He always praises me behind my back. And yet he's much cleverer than me with his hands."

His hands shook as he put the butter on the table. The pile of feathers on the newspaper was growing larger. His brother looked very clean and sparkling with health and vigour. The kettle on the fire began to sing.

"The kettle's boiling," said his mother, infuriatingly. Malcolm shifted the Wild Western away from where the teapot would go. It showed a picture of Wild Bill Hickok blasting away at a rather badly drawn villain in a black hat. He could see that the top corner of page six was drawn down.

"Don't get tea all over that," said Colin.

Malcolm shifted the book over to the dresser. They sat down to their tea. The cock with the twisted neck lay on the paper, on which there was a lot of thick red blood. His brother seemed to have completely forgotten about it, as he cut through a fat scone and spread margarine on it.

[4]

AT NINE O'CLOCK he was still sitting at the table, his mother busying herself with the preparing of the dinner for the following day. She moved about very quietly in the kitchen. Sometimes he sensed that she was watching him, wondering perhaps about the things he was studying, and quite locked away from them. The only subject she could help him with was Gaelic, for she knew old proverbs and old idioms and expressions. One of her favourite sayings was: "Keep a thing seven years and you will find a use for it."

Brooding in the light, he turned over another page. He read: "It has already been shown that positive purpose may be indicated by the relative with subjunctive. E.g., legati missi sunt qui pacem peterent."

He went back over the sentence again. "Ambassadors were sent who asked for peace." "Ambassadors were sent to ask for peace." Each ambassador with his relative subjunctive in attendance. Clearly, through the convolutions of his brain, intertwined with the ambassadors who were asking for peace, he could hear the music from the dance at the end of the road. He imagined Big Dan with the melodeon resting on his knees in the light of the moon, the moon which was ripe and red in the sky. He heard the whoops of the dancers, boys and girls spinning around in the light. "Ambassadors were sent to ask for peace."

He stared unseeingly at the words. He thought of his mother standing many years ago at a fish barrel with the

19

herring in her hand, the salty wind biting in from the sea, her gloves flesh-coloured. He imagined her rising in the darkness of dawn, to make her way with the rest of the girls through the chill reddening air. He heard the terse harsh English voice of the curer. All the girls were young in their lemony rubbery smocks and their long skirts.

"What place was it you were at again when you were at the fishing?" he asked.

His mother looked at him in amazement. "What are you asking that for? You get on with your lesson."

Then she said, as if unwillingly and with a kind of pride :

"Yarmouth," her mouth loosening, as if she were thinking of something pleasant, almost as if she were dreaming.

Another whoop could be heard out of the moonlit night.

"The relative with subjunctive is also used to express consequence or result, more commonly used after one of the following : dignus, worthy; indignus, unworthy . . ."

"Did you like the fishing?" he asked.

"What questions tonight. You should be at your Latin. Mr MacMillan will be angry if you don't know your Latin."

Mr MacMillan was a distant cousin of theirs, a quiet slow gentleman, of whom she was inordinately proud but whom the children called Soppy.

"I don't have Mr MacMillan this year," Malcolm said, unwillingly as if making a concession.

"And you never told me. You never tell me anything. Everyone thinks I'm a fool. There's Mrs Mackenzie and she hasn't got a son in the school and she knows more about it than I do."

He felt a great weariness and through it said : "It's Mr Collins we have this year. I'm doing Higher Latin this year. Mr Collins does Higher Latin."

"Doesn't Mr MacMillan do Higher Latin then?"

"No."

She put this away in her brain as one puts money in a purse against a rainy day. Then :

"Yes. I liked the fishing, but mind you you had your work to do."

She sat down on the stool, a woman of fifty years old, thin, with a thin drooping nose.

"Why can't I go to the dancing?" said Malcolm.

"You? Go to the dancing? You've got your work to do. You're going to university, my lad. Mr Macrae told me that you have to go to the university and no nonsense."

The music was clearer now and he could imagine his brother Colin with his arm round that girl with the red hair and the pale face. The thought disgusted him.

"The relative with subjunctive is also used to express consequence or result most commonly used after one or other . . ."

"Did you go to the dancing when you were young?" he asked, looking up and taking a walk to the door.

"Where are you going?" said his mother.

"For a breath of fresh air." He opened the door and looked out. The sky was astoundingly clear with that red ripe moon so close to earth it was almost like a balloon that someone had hung out. Everything was wet with dew. The plank across the road was white with light and the road itself moonlit as it wound its way towards the dancers. He could hear the pounding of their feet on the road. Oh God, this night of terrifying beauty. The immensity of it! The boys and girls in each others' arms.

"Ambassadors were sent to ask for peace."

He could hear the gurgling of the distant river. On the sea there were some lights.

He turned back into the room and shut the door firmly. And where was Janet now? Was she dancing at some road end in the neighbouring village, locked in someone's arms, laughing up into his face. His mother looked at him worriedly as he came in and sat down at the table again, her stringy throat twisting round to watch him.

"Cicero dignus est qui consul fiat."

He closed the book, picked up the Western and looked at it, listening to the music and leafing through the first page.

"The man on the horse looked down from the brow of the hill onto Dodge City. He had come a long way and now he had reached his goal. Below him in that town was the man he had vowed vengeance on that night three months ago when his kid brother had been gunned down on the sidewalk of a small western town. He stood up straight in his stirrups, his keen blue eyes scanning the whole area around him. Satisfied he . . ."

He closed the Western and picked up his geometry book.

"In a triangle ABC whose mid points are D, E and F . . ."

He began to work, absorbed in his task while the clock ticked on, his mother now looking at him in a more satisfied way. He wrote: "Let the two lines AB and AC be produced to . . ."

His gaze concentrated. The music faded away. The world became a set of straight lines unbroken by moonlight. The cock was cooking gently in the pan on the fire. A kind of simmering was set up in his brain.

His mother was listening to the music which reminded her vaguely of her youth. She was wondering what time Colin would be in. She was wondering what coat she would wear at church the following day. She had only two coats but thought she would wear the black one with the ruff.

She was thinking: He will become a teacher or a minister and then let Mrs Campbell look out. She was thinking: I wish I had been clever in school.

The world of the school and the world of the village didn't meet. The school was twelve miles away and he travelled by bus every morning, returning home in the evening. All the good scholars from the outlying villages attended the big secondary school, standing old and tall and brown-fronted among the trees and leaves on the outskirts of the town. He had friends in the village and some in the school but they never met. When he was at school he could talk about his Highers: when he was in the village he would talk about fish and peats; and football. The only common factor was that he played football in both. Every morning at eight o'clock he would make his way to the bus, climbing an old wall and an old fence on the way, till he came to where the bus would pick him up.

Apart from the pupils there were regulars on the bus who went to town to work. At the beginning of the war there had been Dabby who worked in an insurance office. He would sit beside Dolina, a tall pale girl with spots whose livelihood, such as it was, was gained in an agricultural office. Whenever she came into the bus Dabby would put his hand on the seat below her bottom and laugh out loud. He was the kind of person who always had a new joke. One day he would have a joke about an Irishman, another day one about a Scotsman, for he was not a racialist.

"Did you hear this one?" he'd say, and there would be a universal roar of derision and contempt from all the scholars, making the driver, the conscientious Norry, turn round in the tall red-leathered seat and look at them with his grave gentle face.

"I'll tell you," said Dabby, "there was this Irishman, see, and he was in the First World War and he was making his way to the front. So he was walking along and he heard the firing, see, and he saw the flashes and he didn't like it. So this Colonel came up just as Paddy was running away for all he was worth and this Colonel, see, sitting on a white horse he looked down at Paddy and he said: 'And where are you going, my good man? Don't you know that your place is among the fighting?' And Paddy turned to him—very pale you understand—and said: 'Fighting, bejasus, they're killing each other.' "

And he'd roar with laughter while the scholars would look at him with simulated scorn. Actually, Malcolm quite liked that joke.

Norry didn't like Dabby. He thought he was a bad influence. Norry himself was a serious spectacled man who did some lay-preaching in the evenings and on Sundays. He wore a watch with a chain, and his hair was always perfectly combed back from a high but rather wrinkled forehead. It was fun on the bus. There was always laughter and shouting and argument. Malcolm liked the bus. The other passengers didn't like it because they said it was too noisy. He remembered quite well the day the war broke out. He was coming home across the field, having climbed the fence, and the corn was ripe and golden, the red flowers growing in it, and he was swinging his satchel over his arm. And he saw Tinker with the scythe in his hand, the great wicked blade flashing in the sun, setting up semaphoric signals.

He signed for Malcolm to come over, and came up to him very close, so that Malcolm could see the teeth discoloured with the chewing of tobacco.

"Did you hear?" he said, speaking in a half whisper,

some spittle at the corner of his mouth. "Did you hear?" he said. "The war's started." Malcolm looked at him in amazement and a secret joy. He didn't know what to say, his bag full of Latin books.

"Ay," said Tinker slowly and with relish, "they'll be going away right enough. Ay, the lot will be going away and then we won't see the end of it in a hurry." He looked down at the crooked scythe as into a mirror.

It was such a fine day too, such a fine blue day. Malcolm didn't know what it all meant, except that he thought it would be fun, as everything was fun on the bus. It would be like something out of P. C. Wren, heroism and high adventure.

The following day Dabby said: "Well, lads, I'll be off after the Nazis soon." But behind the jollity of the tone there was the shadow of worry.

Someone shouted: "Bet you'll be like the Irishman." It was meant as a joke, but Dabby burst out: "Ay, you're too young. You've got the best of it. You've got the education. I didn't get any education. You'll be exempt."

There was a silence on the bus, then in a shamefaced manner he muttered: "You'll see me in the cinema, sinking the 'Bismarck'."

Norry didn't say anything. He wouldn't have to go to war because someone must drive the bus. Anyway, he was against war on principle. The New Testament said that we must love one another and, in a way, he was glad to see Dabby leaving. He was an immoral influence, an unchristian person.

One day Norry was carrying an old helmet and a greatcoat in the bus. He had joined the LDV. "I'll be driving the truck for them," he announced, with eyes shining.

Dabby looked at the back of his neck for a moment and

then said: "Ay, old Norry will keep you safe. He'll look
after you, make sure that you don't miss your Latin. When
the Germans are finished with France and want a bit of
fishing they'll come here and Norry will show them the
best parts with his truck."

Dabby did join the Navy and was drowned six months
afterwards on convoy duty.

Malcolm used to take his dinner with a relative of his
mother's, who stayed in a tenement. He would take slices of
bread with him and they would supply his tea. Instead of
sugar he would use saccharine. There were no sweets to be
had except on coupons. Books too were scarce though sometimes he might buy one or two in Woolworths. He would
buy the *Listener* and try the crossword, but he could
hardly ever do it. He hated going to his relatives for lunch
and sitting there with his sandwiches, while the others were
having a proper meal. Though they often invited him to
share it, he didn't like to.

On the mantelpiece there was a weather thing and
when the day was fine a man and a woman dressed in
Dutch clothing and with round apple cheeks would come
out; but when the weather was wet they didn't come out
at all. They reminded him a bit of his two relatives, the
man and the wife.

Food was scarce in those days but sometimes he would
buy kippers and salt fish and take them home. He didn't
like doing messages, but he seemed to be always doing
them while his brother did very few. They bought fresh
butter at a house about a mile away, paying two shillings
for a pound. The man of the house was a fisherman and
the wife was small, brisk and kind. They had only one
daughter and no sons. The name of the daughter was
Sheila and she was small and dark, about a year younger

than himself. Sometimes on a Saturday night he would get milk for Sunday morning and play draughts with the old fisherman while Sheila watched the two of them. She herself didn't play, but seemed to be interested, and her father and mother were quite happy to see her watching the game.

It was fine on the bus on a summer morning when he would stand on the deck waiting to jump off, his open-necked shirt stirring in the breeze. He liked jumping off when the bus was going at great speed and often wished Janet could see him. Though she belonged to one of the outlying villages, Janet didn't travel by bus but stayed in the Girl's Hostel. Norry didn't like him doing this for he was responsible if anything happened, but there Malcolm was, hanging out, swinging on the silvery bar as the bus careered round the corner. Dabby had once told a joke about it.

"Did you hear about the hunchback on the bus?" he said. "Well, there was this hunchback and he was waiting on the deck of the bus to get off and there were others behind him. And one of them said to the hunchback as the bus was drawing up, you know he said to him : 'Hurry up man, what are you waiting for?' And the hunchback said, do you know what he said? He said—pointing to his back, you see—'What do you think this is? A parachute?' "

Norry thought this was shameful, absolutely shameful, especially as he himself had a brother who was a bit hunch-backed. The sooner Dabby was away in the war the better. They'd sort him out there, he thought virtuously. But then he was doing his bit, too : the LDV was a useful organisation and one of these days they'd teach him how to fire a rifle. He might be able to kill a rabbit now and then. His wife would like a rabbit for her Sunday dinner, freshly killed.

5

"WHAT DO YOU mean by it?" said Mr Twigg, staring hard at Malcolm, his little red eyes burning in his pale face, and flecks of foam on his lips. "What do you mean by it?"

Malcolm swallowed but said nothing.

"I have never, never, never," said Mr Twigg, "never seen anything so scandalous in all my days. I wouldn't have believed it possible. Not possible."

He slammed his finger down so hard on the paper that he seemed to wrench it. He went a deeper shade of pale but showed no other sign of the pain.

"If you had only written something pleasant, something moral, something decent, such as W. H. Davies might have written, something humorous, something healthy and pleasant, suitable for a school magazine in those days of shortage of paper. I'm not against humour; no one can say I'm against humour—in its place—but this is an offence against the dead. You are lucky, I tell you you are lucky, that I have decided not to report you to the rector and that only because of your record, because of your previous record, before this aberration."

His moustache quivered, the hairs like antennae, searching.

"I cannot understand that you ... one of my best pupils, one of my best pupils at interpretation, and also at the descriptive essay, should have written this. I do not and cannot understand. Well, what do you say? What have you to say?"

In truth, Malcolm couldn't understand how he should have written it. And yet he had. And he had enjoyed writing it, too.

He wanted to wipe the specks of foam from his face, but didn't.

"Anyway, it can't go on. And you a member of the committee! Setting such an example. What if the younger children had read it, eh? I am ashamed of you. Ashamed. Ashamed of you."

The face seemed to pale even more, and for a moment Malcolm thought that Mr Twigg was going to faint, for the latter put his hand to his chest, shaking. Mr Twigg turned away, gesturing speechlessly while he slipped a white pill into his mouth.

Malcolm slunk off.

They crowded round him. On the rim of the ring he saw Janet, looking at him and laughing darkly.

"What happened? What was that in aid of?" said Neil. Neil was the scientist of the class, best at physics, chemistry and mathematics. He had a dark competent air and would probably be an engineer.

"C-come on," stuttered fat Jerry, "what was it all about, eh?" his slobbery body shaking, his glasses glittering, his loose mouth avid for scandal.

"An article I wrote," said Malcolm, airily. He looked down at his flannels and at the shadow he cast on the earth, in front of the dappled wall. Miriam was watching him too with her trim neat gaze, in her long white pleated skirt.

"What was it?" they insisted. "What was it about? It must have been bad."

"It was just an imitation of In Memoriams."

Now that he came to think of it, the article hadn't been all that good.

"What?"

"I just took all the In Memoriams you get in the paper and I did a take off. That's all."

He looked carefully down at his brown shoes, watching Janet out of the corner of his eye. Her black hair stirred in the breeze, her face tanned as a Red Indian's.

She stood there, her arm resting lightly on the shoulder of another girl. To be so beautiful. What must it be like to be so beautiful? To wake up and know that you were beautiful. To know that all the people would bow and kneel to you. To be so continually desired. To know that your every movement was followed by eyes of lust. What was it like to live in such a world? To watch yourself endlessly in a mirror.

"Tell us one," said Jerry, rapturously. "Tell us one before the bell goes. Go on."

That fat slob, that fat clever slob, Jerry.

"All right," he said, carelessly. "They're not going to be printed anyway."

He struck an attitude:

> *To think we'll never see your face*
> *as we did see of yore*
> *when you would come at eventide*
> *so happy through the door.*

"That was one of them," he said, in a shamefaced way. It didn't really sound so good.

"How disgusting," said Miriam, walking away with a flounce. "Disgusting," flicking her pony tail angrily.

Some of the others burst out laughing. Janet looked at him with what seemed to be admiration.

She came forward. "You mean," she said, "that you handed that in to Mr Twigg?"

There seemed to be a dew on her lips.

"Yes," he answered joyously, the hero.

She laughed. "Well, good for you."

But there was a puzzlement in her laughter.

"Another one," stuttered Jerry. "Have you another one?"

"Well, I don't . . ."

Really, this was going a bit far. And they weren't as good as that, when you studied them closely. He said:

> *There always is a vacant space*
> *where once there was your seat*
> *and we will love you more and more*
> *though we can't see your feet.*

Jerry went into a fat paroxysm of laughter, his whole face seeming to disintegrate. Neil smiled coolly. After a while, Jerry took off his glasses and began to polish them with a dirty handkerchief.

"What did Old Twiggy say?" said Neil.

"Oh, he nearly had hysterics," said Malcolm casually. "I thought he was going to drop dead in front of me. He took a pill."

Suddenly little James pushed forward and said furtively: "You know, when I was in first year he sent me to a chemist's shop for stomach . . . stomach powders."

They all burst out laughing, thinking of this and also thinking of being in first year.

Janet came up to him: "You shouldn't have said that, you know," she said.

31

Her eyes glinted as if she were testing him.

"What?" he asked. "Shouldn't have said what?"

"Didn't you know that Miriam lost her father recently?"

Funny how when Janet said this she seemed to be triumphing over him, as if she wanted to defeat him in his moment of glory.

"Is that true?" he asked excitedly. "Is that true?" But at the same moment he put on his armour of callousness. "I didn't know about that. I mean, it wasn't against her . . ."

"Of course it wasn't," said Jerry, his eyes glinting as well. "It took g-guts you know to do that. Anyway, it's just satire. It's not meant for her."

One of the girls said: "Jerry doesn't mind if old Twigg puts you off the committee. He wants to get on it himself."

"That's dirty, that's dirty," said Jerry hysterically. "That's dirty."

"I think he's leaving me on the committee," said Malcolm, thinking about Miriam running away in her long white skirt, her pony tail tossing.

The bell rang and they all walked away, except for Janet who waited. With his heart in his mouth he said to her:

"I'll get you a piece of turnip this afternoon."

She didn't say anything, not even signifying that she had heard him. But all the time he was thinking of Miriam running away and saying: "Disgusting", and that fat Jerry who wanted to be on the committee himself, and who might get a good bursary all because he was good at French and German.

He wished he could be like Neil, who hardly ever spoke; the strong silent man, the Horatio who would have a pipe in his mouth as he told his underlings where the struts of the bridge were to be put, somewhere in India perhaps.

And there was himself shooting off his mouth and he couldn't even understand why he had done it.

Suddenly, he blurted out: "Do you think it was wrong?"

She looked at him, mockingly, and said: "It was very clever. But I must hurry. We've got gym."

The wind moved over her dress. The shadows played on her face. The sun shone all round her. Persephone. And in a moment he had forgotten about Mr Twigg. His flannels fluttered in the breeze and he wanted to be playing football, racing down the wing, devious, cunning, the studs of his boots like eagles' claws, the ball soaring towards the net beyond outstretched hands, and Janet watching him.

"I'm not sorry," he shouted, but by that time it was too late.

She was gone in a burst of yellow flame.

6

Malcolm would often go and visit Dicky, who had come home from the Army with TB and was dying from it. Malcolm was terrified of TB—of the visible wasting whiteness, like a candle guttering—but nevertheless he forced himself to go. The two of them would play draughts: so far he hadn't won a game against Dicky. He knew there was a lot of haemorrhaging in TB and in fact Dicky had been taken off the ship in a stretcher, haemorrhaging badly, and this terrified Malcolm so much that one night he had wakened up in the bed beside his brother, feeling that he was being choked by blood. His brother hadn't even wakened, his skull yellow in the moonlight. Before Dicky had taken to his bed, he and Malcolm would walk along the road in the warm summer evenings. On these evenings they would reach the corner of the road before turning back, and would discuss books and local gossip; anything but the war. Though Dicky had left school at fifteen he was very intelligent and had read modern books.

This particular afternoon Dicky was sitting in a chair, wrapped in a muffler, though it was quite warm outside where the cows were munching the grass round the house and the butterflies swooped after each other, above the white and red flowers. The sea's lazy swell could be seen moving towards the shore. Malcolm didn't like entering the dark house of imminent death after the brightness of the sunshine, but he did.

"How are you today?" he asked cheerfully, sitting down in a chair opposite Dicky.

"Not too bad," said Dicky, through the white muffler, his voice husky. There was something wrong with his throat. Dicky's mother always welcomed Malcolm: his father was working in a mill.

"And how is your mother today?" asked Dicky's mother. She was a thin, dark, nervous looking woman, who seemed to have partially surrendered to whatever nightmare or tragedy was about to hit her and which was already investing the house, tightening its grip mindlessly. Her gaze could almost be described as scattered.

"Fine, Mrs Morrison," said Malcolm, as if apologising.

"That's good," she answered, as if it were extraordinary and at the same time irritating that other people should be well when her son was so ill. At times she deluded herself into thinking that he would get well and for this reason was always feeding him milk and porridge.

"Have you got the draughtboard?" said Malcolm, in the same cheerful voice which seemed to ring hollowly through the house, echoing among the dead white ornaments, which included a bouquet of marblish flowers and a gipsy's cart full of needles.

Without answering, Dicky got the board and pieces out from a drawer, which was set in the table.

Malcolm was frightened that Mrs Morrison would offer him tea. He didn't like eating and drinking in the house in case he got germs. For this reason he always came over just after he had had a meal.

"What are you reading?" he asked Dicky, who held up a book with a dark red cover: it might have been a Penguin. He had a quick look at the names: Auden, Day Lewis, Chamfort. While Dicky was setting up the pieces his eye was caught by the Auden poem, which he rapidly skimmed through. He had been attracted by the opening lines which were:

> *Easily, my dear, you move, easily your head*
> *And easily as through the leaves of a photograph*
> *   album I'm led ...*

"I like the C. Day Lewis one," said Dicky.

Malcolm didn't answer. His eye had been caught by another verse:

> *The power that corrupts, that power to excess*
> *The beautiful quite naturally possess:*
> *To them the fathers and the children turn:*
> *And all who long for their destruction,*
> *The arrogant and self-insulted wait*
> *   The looked instruction.*

What did that mean? But these lines! "The power which corrupts, that power to excess, The beautiful quite naturally possess ..."

He laid the book down on the table.

"Auden is good, isn't he?" he said in wonderment.

"There's a good one by C. Day Lewis," said Dicky.

"Where?"

"It's not in that one. It's in another one. It's called 'The Conflict'."

"I think that poem by Auden is very good," said Malcolm, again in wonderment, thinking "The power which corrupts, that power to excess, The beautiful quite naturally possess."

It was right enough, dead right. Accurate.

Mrs Morrison was still standing at the door and she said to Malcolm:

"It's chilly today, isn't it?" Malcolm looked at Dicky's muffler and said, "Yes, it is, quite. It's not so warm as it was yesterday," though the sky was cloudless.

"Well, I'll leave you two to get on with your draughts," said Mrs Morrison, and went off into the other room, perhaps to sew or knit or brood or whatever she did.

"Toss for white," said Dicky, in the same hoarse voice.

"Yes, all right," said Malcolm. Dicky took out a florin and won the toss.

"I think we should learn chess sometime," said Malcolm, carelessly. "They say it's a difficult game."

"They say that," said Dicky, bending to the board. He played a flank game always and this game was no exception. He played white on the right flank. Malcolm studied the board and after a while he played black on the right flank as well. He felt the sunlight lying on his warm right hand and when he looked down there was a mottling of white and black on it, like some kind of foliage.

Dicky coughed behind his hand, a small dry cough. He played towards the right flank again. Malcolm did the same, looking covertly at Dicky, whose face had in the previous weeks become very thin, the cheeks sunken with a small red spot on each and the upper lip disfigured by a cold scab.

Dicky sipped delicately from a tumbler of milk as he played to the right flank again. Malcolm wondered whether he should start sacrificing, in order to break up the movement on the right, but decided that he would duplicate the last movement as well. Both forces were now aligned along the right flank. It was up to Dicky whether he should sacrifice on his right flank. This in fact was what he did.

While studying the board, Malcolm said: "Anything good in any of your Penguin *New Writings*?"

"There's a short story by Rex Warner," said Dicky, coughing again slightly.

"What's it about?"

"I'm not sure. It's strange."

For a moment Dicky's eyes stared across at him with a keen glitter. Malcolm almost felt hate in them. Then they clouded over and dimmed and became gentle, as if he had been struggling against some powerful force.

As he turned his eyes back to the board again, Malcolm was wondering what it was like to be dying. Did Dicky know that he was dying? He probably did. There was an unshaven look about the face, too. In the past, Dicky had always been very neat and well groomed. Perhaps the unshaven appearance was a sign that the will was surrendering. He remembered that before going to the war Dicky had been quite a good footballer, graceful and clever.

Suddenly Malcolm said: "I don't understand how England can keep that team together, Matthews, Carter and Lawton. They're never sent on war service, are they? They're never out of England."

It was a sore point with him that the English were winning all the football internationals, sometimes by scores as high as 7-1.

"They're pretty good," said Dicky. "You can't stop Matthews," he added, coughing again behind his hand. "I saw him once."

"You mean in the flesh?"

"Yes, at Wembley. I saw a game there. Jock Shaw couldn't stop him. He hadn't an earthly."

Malcolm looked at him with renewed respect.

"Imagine that," he said, "seeing him in the flesh. Is he that good?"

"He's the best I've seen," said Dicky, "and I saw Finney too."

Malcolm moved a black from the back row to strengthen his flank.

"What do you think of that?" he said, cheerfully and falsely. He was instantly aware that Mrs Morrison was again standing in the doorway. She nodded to him approvingly and vanished.

Dicky studied the board and eventually moved a white piece from his back row to strengthen his flank.

"Hm," said Malcolm, in an exaggerated way as if talking to a child. "Hm, I see what you're at."

Dicky smiled faintly. Malcolm had never beaten him and he wanted to. He didn't like losing at draughts because it was a game that he enjoyed playing. The thought suddenly came to him : "I hope I beat him once before he ..." The thought was pushed down abruptly, squirming and wriggling like a fish at the end of a hook.

He moved a right flank piece back towards the middle. The position was quite reasonable. He leaned back in his chair and began to whistle. Then he stopped, because he would be breathing air into his lungs and there might be germs. He leaned forward.

The game continued. As he was playing, Malcolm was listening to the sound of the cows munching, to the swell of the sea and the hum of the insects. Dicky was as if carved from stone, except that now and then he would cough a little and tighten his lips against each other.

"I don't think I'll ever beat him," said Malcolm to himself. "This is all he has." Suddenly he realised it fully : "This is all he has." And then he thought : perhaps I ought to let him win again, but he wouldn't do that out of respect for Dicky, and also because he wanted to win. But the game was very close and he had manoeuvred himself almost by chance into a strong position. He completely forgot himself, lost in the board, and listening now and then to that cough, on the edge of his consciousness.

Without warning, the words came into his mind again:

"That power to excess, the beautiful quite naturally possess."

He opened the Penguin *New Writing* which was lying beside him:

> *Certain it became while we were still incomplete*
> *There were certain prizes for which we would never*
> *   compete.*
> *A choice was killed by every childish illness,*
> *The boiling tears among the hothouse plants,*
> *The rigid promise fractured in the garden,*
> *   And the long aunts.*

Dicky made his move and looked up at Malcolm, his eyes beginning to glitter again. Malcolm looked down at the board and knew he had lost.

"Ah well," he said, inwardly seething, "you've won again. I can't see you losing now. You're like Matthews. I can't stop you." He looked at the small green clock. "I'll give you ten minutes to finish it off and then I'll have to go." Dicky looked at him without saying anything. It occurred to Malcolm that hardly anyone else came to see him.

> *But be my good,*
> *Daily, nightly*

The game was over in less than the ten minutes. Malcolm got to his feet.

"I'll come and see you next Saturday, or perhaps a night during the week if I don't have much homework."

Dicky leaned back and took another sip of milk, nodding his head and looking down at the board. He began slowly to put the pieces back in the box. The game had taken a lot out of him.

"Look after yourself," said Malcolm, with false bonhomie, "and we might get out for a walk one of these days."

He felt very moved and pleased with himself that he had got another visit over.

He looked down at Dicky's bent head. "Cheerio just now."

He moved out into the sunshine, getting away before Mrs Morrison could offer him tea.

He began to run through the warm day, jumping and cavorting as he left the shadow of the house and entered the sunshine. He jumped a ditch and rushed up to his own house, travelling like the wind.

7

AFTER LEAVING DICKY he went and sought out
Dell, whom he found sitting on a wall, carving a wooden
duck with a knife.

"Want a game?" he said.

Dell immediately swung himself down from the wall
and they went off together up the brae, over the bed of the
dried stream, to the full-sized football pitch laid out with
goalposts, though there were no nets.

As they were walking along Dell said, "Saw Peggy
today."

"Where?"

"In a cornfield with Danny," said Dell, spitting reflectively on the ground. "They never saw me. I watched
them. Wished I had spying glasses."

"What were they doing?" said Malcolm, with a thrill of
delight.

"What do you think? Their arms were round each
other, and they were lying down. What do you think?"

Dell himself went about with Sheila, who lived in the
house where Malcolm bought the butter. She was the
small dark rank girl who was rather like Peggy: Peggy
worked in a shop.

Dell would soon start work as a cook on a fishing boat
when he had finished school, as he would that year. He
was in Colin's class: neither of them did a stroke of work
and were simply waiting till they could leave a building
which was becoming more and more unreal for them.

"Lawton's a great footballer," said Malcolm suddenly. "He's great with the head, isn't he?"

"I like Carter better," said Dell. Then, a bit later: "There's none of them to touch Alan Morton. They called him the Blue Devil," he added.

They climbed the brae on the opposite side of the stream till they came to the football field.

"Got the cork?" said Dell.

For answer, Malcolm took it out of his pocket. It was an ordinary fishing cork whose great disadvantage as a football was that it screwed away at an angle when you hit it. They had no football. At one time they had a glossy rainbow-coloured ball but it had disappeared.

"Pitch is dry," said Dell, bending down and feeling it with his hand.

"Toss for sides?" They tossed, and Malcolm won.

They placed the cork in the centre of the field and began to play. They could keep this up for an hour if necessary on a full-sized football pitch, but it was hard going and they would be sweating like pigs before they were finished.

Whenever Malcolm got to the football pitch he immediately forgot about everything except the game. He played right-footed and wished sometimes that he could use his left foot, but he didn't have the patience to practise with it. The difficulty about playing on a full-sized football pitch was that after about twenty minutes, when one of them got past the other, there was no point in trying to run after him so Malcolm usually tried to conserve his energies.

Dell was allowed to kick off. He tried to flick the ball through Malcolm's legs but the latter, anticipating this, had brought his boots together and caught the cork between them. He flicked the cork to the right and began to run down the right wing, Dell trying to force him over the touchline.

When he was playing, Malcolm thought of himself as Willie Waddell or Gordon Smith. Which one he was depended on what he preferred at the time. If he was in favour of skill he preferred Smith, if in favour of strength he preferred Waddell. Today he was in favour of Smith. He imagined himself graceful in green with white cuffs against a sky of deepest blue, his thin jersey winking in the wind. Forced over to the right he swung abruptly to the left, though this was awkward for him, and warding off a challenge from Dell he moved into the centre. As Dell lumbered after him he suddenly stopped dead, holding the cork under his foot. Dell careered past. He himself took the cork over to his right foot and hit it as hard as he could, but it veered past the goalpost.

Dell placed the cork inside the penalty area and began to dribble out, eye over the cork as he had been taught. He swung over to the right, passed Malcolm and kept on going up the touchline. Suddenly he unleashed a terrific shot to gain ground and the two of them raced for the cork but Malcolm was faster and beat him to it, giving away a corner. Dell placed the ball at the corner flag (or where the corner flag would have been had there been one) and began to dribble outwards. He kicked suddenly and tried to round Malcolm but Malcolm stuck out a foot, stopped the cork and began to run as fast as he could down the right wing, his jersey billowing in the slight breeze. Now he could sense fluidity and power in his whole body, now he was impregnated with purpose and poise, now he could hear the phantom cheers from ten thousand throats; his legs suddenly blossomed with real football stockings and real shinguards. The right foot was controlling the cork. He flicked it forward, holding it as it veered over to the right, came into the penalty area and dribbled it casually into the open goal.

One up.

He ran back to the centre as footballers always did, looking down at the ground and feeling proud and humble at the same time. He had thought for a moment of leaving the cork at Dell's goal as professional footballers did but thought that this would be rather unsporting and excessive in the context. Dell began again. The trouble with him was that he had no fresh ideas. Again he tried to flick the cork between Malcolm's legs and again Malcolm stopped it. This time he held it and tried to do the same thing to Dell. He flicked the cork between Dell's legs, sprinted round him and got away before Dell could catch up. He tried gallantly to catch Malcolm but was too late.

Two up.

By this time they were both puffing and blowing, their faces white and strained. But neither wanted to be the first to ask for half time. Dell centred again. Malcolm managed to stop the cork but his foot caught in the turf and the cork swung away from him. Dell seized on it immediately and using his left foot brought it under control, ran up the touchline before Malcolm could catch him and scored easily.

Without a word being spoken they sat down on the turf, signifying half time.

After a while, Dell said: "You going to play for the school?"

Malcolm picked up a blade of grass, put it in his mouth and said: "I might."

"You should play for the village," said Dell, the splotches of red still on his face.

45

"I don't know," said Malcolm. "I'd like to play for the school. They travel more."

Of course, that wasn't the real reason. The real reason was that playing for the school was more glamorous and they had better strips, claret coloured with white cuffs.

"I think you should play for the village," Dell insisted, and added, almost reluctantly : "You're pretty fast."

Dell himself would be playing for the village and, in fact, the two teams would be meeting soon in a cup game.

"I'd play for the village if I was you," said Dell; and then : "You should have seen Sheila the other night. I nearly . . ."

He stopped talking, looking slyly at Malcolm who felt slightly disgusted yet thrilled at this talk.

"It was coming home from the bus," said Dell. "I put my hand on her breast and she didn't take it away." He continued : "Jimmy was saying he was with her in the cemetery one night." He stopped chewing and kicked viciously at a stone. "Wish I'd got proper football boots," he said, "yellow ones." Then he lay down flat on his back and looked up at the sky. "Another time," he said, "we were round at the privy behind the school you know. She's got garters. I saw her garters. They're pink. She sits just in front of me in the class."

He smiled into the sky contemplatively, his hair tousled, one leg crossed over the other.

"She goes to the flicks two nights a week, you know. I think you should play for the village," he added, again standing above Malcolm, who was thinking about Gordon Smith and wishing he also had a pair of yellow football boots.

He was also thinking of Janet and wondering if he could ask her to go to the pictures with him. Somehow, Sheila and Janet seemed to belong to two different worlds.

He had a feeling that Dell was not telling the truth about Sheila. She would never go to the high—she would always stay in the village school—but she was sensitive too in her way, and ambitious. He shut his eyes, feeling the heat of the sun on them.

"One more goal," he said. "We'll stop whoever gets the first goal. It's hot."

They lined up again (if one could use such a term) opposite each other and this time it was Malcolm's turn to start. He feinted with the cork instead of kicking it, drew Dell over to the left and then swung over to the right. Dell recovered himself quickly and came in with a heavy shoulder charge, throwing him to the ground as the cork went into touch. Malcolm felt resentfully at his shoulder, looking up at Dell panting above him, his huge hairy legs like columns, with the stockings fallen down to his boots.

"Hey," he said, "watch what you're doing."

But Dell didn't say anything, his face white and determined. After a while he did speak :

"A fair charge," he said.

"That's what they do to Matthews and Gordon Smith," said Malcolm, complainingly. "They cut them down."

"If you play against us for the school," said Dell, "I'll do it then too. It's fair enough. Fair warning."

They glared at each other. Malcolm placed the cork on the touchline, diddled about without touching it, pretended to swing right and then kicked the cork through Dell's legs. He rounded him quickly, running at great speed, not wanting to be charged again, held it, kicked it forward as far as he could, then swung in on goal before the cork could over-run the touchline. He kicked the cork into the empty goalmouth and raised his hands above his head in the gesture of victory.

"That's it," he shouted triumphantly.

"Another one," said Dell.

"No, we agreed," said Malcolm, stubbornly. "We agreed."

"Go on. Another goal," said Dell.

"No, I told you we agreed. Fair's fair."

"All right," said Dell walking away, "it's your cork."

"That's got nothing to do with it." Dell's gipsy cheeks flushed.

"It's got everything to do with it." He clenched his hands against his side.

They walked along in silence for a while and then, in an impulse of friendship, Malcolm put his hand on Dell's shoulder but Dell turned away.

"Want to play for the village?" he asked.

"No," said Malcolm.

By the time they had climbed the other side of the stream they were on friendly terms again.

When Malcolm got home Colin said to him, "I've been picked for the village team."

Malcolm looked at him in surprise, for Colin wasn't really a very good footballer. In fact, he was pretty plodding, though fanatically fond of the game.

"Good for you," said Malcolm, unlacing his boots.

"Do you want to go to the dance tonight?" said Colin.

"No," said Malcolm, without thinking. "I've got homework."

"Have you a good team in the school?" said Colin, looking speculatively into the mirror.

"Yes, pretty good, We've got a chap called Ronny Black. He's centre forward. He's pretty good. And Murdo MacMillan, outside left. They're about the best."

"Aside from yourself?"

"Aside from myself," said Malcolm, laughing. "Have you finished that Wild Western yet?"

"No. It's not very good. Not enough action. What's that Latin stuff like?"

"Hard," said Malcolm, "pretty hard." He filled a basin with water to wash his feet.

"Old Thorny once asked me if I wanted to take Latin," said Colin. "Imagine that." He laughed in a way that was half dismissive, half honoured.

"Yes," said Malcolm, "I know that. He always does that in first year." Casually he asked. "What position are you playing?"

"Left half."

Malcolm didn't say anything else. He knew his brother was a defensive player but he thought he would have been better on the right as he couldn't use his left foot very well. They were only playing him on the left because it was difficult to get left-footed players anyway, and there would be plenty of better players for the right side of the field. It was very odd that Malcolm should be a better footballer than Colin since Colin was much more agile than him in most ways.

"I'm sure you'll keep your place," said Malcolm, reaching out for a piece of sackcloth with which to dry his feet. "I saw Dicky this afternoon." He gazed at his feet, which were curiously white and vulnerable like feet seen in a mediaeval picture.

"Oh?" said Colin, combing his hair at the mirror.

"He's not too well. Why don't you go and see him?"

"I was meaning to but I didn't have the time. I don't know what to say to him."

"What do you mean?"

"Well, he's always reading these books of his."

"I see. Do you never get any homework yourself?" said Malcolm, studying his nails and wondering whether he should cut them or not.

Colin laughed briefly, then turned round and looked at his brother. He really liked Malcolm, though he was a bit of a drip sometimes, and he was rather proud of him. If he envied him for anything it was for his football ability.

At that moment it was curious to see them looking across at each other; Malcolm, thin faced, brown haired, ears slightly projecting, eyes brown and the brow rather narrow, Colin with the wider brow, blue eyes, ginger hair, full lips, roundish face, with the down still on it.

Malcolm looked down at the basin again. Colin stood there with the red comb in his hand. Sometimes, moments like this came to Malcolm, moments of vision when he could see people, himself included, as if in a strange unreal place, as if he were looking across a no man's land. Once he had been walking along the road when he stopped to allow a funeral to pass. It was actually a very long funeral and he could see the hexagonal yellow coffin quite clearly. However, there was no funeral that day, as he had found out from his mother. He had been extremely frightened when she had told him this. So it was at this moment, raising his face and watching his brother with the comb in his hand. It was almost as if he wished to stretch his hand across a great divide which he could see rapidly widening and filling with the salt sea.

"We'd better do something about the peats soon," said Colin, as if he were the head of the house.

The spell was snapped.

[8]

ON A SUNDAY afternoon Malcolm would sometimes go down to the seashore or sit on a headland overlooking the water. Often he would take a book with him and lie there on his private promontory, as if overlooking Marathon.

He liked sitting on the headland, watching the ships sail past, metal grey, far out in the water. Sometimes through the haze he could see a convoy going past, half hidden by the heat mist. It was strange to chew a blade of grass and watch these ships. Perhaps on board one of them was a lad from the village, staring desperately towards his own village as the massive ship carried him past it over the ruled water. It was almost like seeing yourself looking back at yourself out of that mirror of exile and longing.

At times he would think of things that had happened to him during that week. For instance, he thought of the Latin teacher, Mr Collins, drawing him aside the previous Tuesday and asking him what subjects he intended taking in the Bursary Competition, which he would be sitting that summer in order to get additional money for university. Mr Collins was a small, quick, brash man who had a forelock of reddish hair falling over the right side of his brow and who spoke like a machine gun. He came into the classroom like a tornado, the book already open in his hand, the other hand closing the door behind him, his large nose like the beak of one of his Roman ships. Rostrum . . .

"Latin's difficult," he was saying. "Latin's not easy, not easy at all. I sat Latin myself in the Bursary Competition. Very different from the Highers. Very different. Standard much higher than the Highers."

He laughed quickly as if he didn't have too much time, not even for laughing, as if he had made a joke, but as if the joke were a concession to barbarism.

"I once got 106 out of 100 in a paper in the university, but I didn't get that in the Bursary Competition. Don't believe me, eh? But it's true. I got 106 marks out of 100. You'll have to work hard, you know. No substitute for hard work. What are the subjects you're thinking of taking?"

"English, mathematics, history, as well as Latin," said Malcolm, sniffing the resin in Mr Collins' small room and gazing at the white head of what could have been Cicero or Vergil.

"Ah, all those people in the war," said Mr Collins abruptly. "When I think of them, my pupils scattered all over the world, over all the oceans of the world, taking the routes which the Romans took, it reminds me of the Punic wars. Yes indeed. Mathematics, eh? Are you good at mathematics? Could you say that you have a talent for mathematics? It is a curious thing that talents for mathematics and Latin go together."

"I like geometry," said Malcolm. This was an understatement. He idolised, adored geometry with the pure love that Plato might have bestowed on his Forms. Geometry to him was the music of the spheres and a solution to a geometrical problem more beautiful than poetry.

"Ah, yes, geometry," said Mr Collins. "Yes, I can quite see that. But geometry is not the whole of mathematics, is it? There will be more than geometry. Eh?"

"I don't know," said Malcolm, "I haven't seen a specimen paper."

"What! Not seen a paper, eh? Not seen a paper. That is inexcusable. That must be looked to at once. But in Latin make sure of your subjunctives. Your Latin into English is passable but your English into Latin must be looked into. Make sure of that. The subjunctive is very important in Latin. For such a practical race the Romans were a very subjunctive people." He laughed again. "You keep at it," and added, leaning forward confidentially: "remember that they may print the 'u's as 'v's. Remember that." He spoke as if somewhere at the centre of things there was an enormous conspiracy, a plot against the alphabet itself. "And don't forget, the war won't go on for ever. Just work. Work hard as you can. That is the true gospel. Otherwise there is darkness."

Malcolm thought of this as he watched the ships cruising past through a haze which was not the fictitious haze of Vergilian days. Wearily, he opened his *Aeneid* and glanced at the section about Dido and Aeneas. He thought of the Mediterranean and then thought of something else.

It had happened the previous winter. There was a boy in the village called Nobby who was serving in the Navy, as indeed were practically all the servicemen in the village. Malcolm had been studying Latin till late and had gone to bed about ten o'clock. He heard, as if in a dream, steps on the gravel outside and then the door being opened. His bed was in the kitchen and through a haze of sleep he heard Nobby's voice. Nobby had come to say goodbye at the end of his leave. All the servicemen did this. When their leave was over they would make a tour of all the houses in the village to say goodbye. Nobby would be leaving on the midnight boat from the town pier. Malcolm heard Nobby's voice and his mother's murmuring in the glare of the Tilley light, so harsh that he couldn't open his eyes against it. The lashes seemed to be stuck together though he could see vaguely the yellow light. After about ten minutes he heard Nobby standing up, and felt him standing at the bed and saying that he didn't want to wake him up. Malcolm made another determined effort to lever the lids of his eyes upward, but he couldn't. It was as if he was drowning in yellow water with the thickness of tar. And all this because of the Latin he had been studying that night. Then he heard Nobby going away, the door opening and shutting amidst a murmur of conversation, then the footsteps on final gravel.

Two weeks later news came that Nobby had been drowned, his cruiser sunk by a submarine in a sea which Nobby probably wouldn't have been able to indicate on a map in the days of his education, such as they had been.

Thinking of Nobby standing by the bed and looking down at him, and imagining the white naval cap, like the top of a wave, with the yellow script on it, Malcolm felt as if he had betrayed Nobby in some way or other. It was as if by indifference he had sent him to his death, as if he had drowned him in that yellow light.

Thoughts such as these flitted into his mind as he watched the convoy sliding past in the endless calm of the day. A butterfly swam lazily past him. He thrust out his hand but the butterfly avoided it. In the distance he could see blue smoke rising from the houses into the clear air. It seemed that the houses of the village were like ships perpetually becalmed in water. There was no movement anywhere, apart from the white butterfly drifting and slanting in the blue air. Sunday had clamped down on the world. The day of God had imprisoned it. He began to think of what Dell had told him of the bodies locked together and wished that he were locked in Janet's arms, leaning over her brown freckled mocking face.

And this led him to think of something else that had happened that week.

He had promised to get Janet a turnip. This was not in fact so comical as one might think, for the school under a patriotic headmaster with a small fierce moustache, who was himself too old for military service, had its own plot of ground where turnips and carrots were grown. If you jumped over a high wall, there on the other side lay the field. The pupils dug the earth in spring, planted their potatoes, turnips and carrots, and harvested them in the autumn. That particular day Malcolm had dug out a beautiful bluish tinged turnip and had hidden it under his jacket. He remembered clearly the quick deft way in which he had snatched it before old Storrie, the Technical teacher, could see him and how he had then climbed the high wall as if escaping from prison. It wasn't really stealing : it was a product of his own work.

At the interval he had gone to Janet and offered her this turnip which he had sliced with a knife. And she had eaten some of it too. He had never had such a sensation in his life. It was as if for the first time he had thought of himself as a husband providing for his wife. It was as if he had entered a new responsible world, which at the same time was of an incredible sweetness. As he saw her eating the turnip, her teeth white against the whiteness of the turnip in the blue sky, he was filled with the most inexpressible joy, rather like that joy he had felt once before when a cousin of theirs on leave from the war had slept in their house. He, Malcolm, had gone to see him sleeping peacefully in their bed, a stranger safe for the moment,

55

unafraid, submitting himself to the shelter of a house not his own, his drawn face, used to war and alarms, at rest. Malcolm had slipped away, trying to control his joy, which was like a pail of water in his hands, balanced precariously, almost spilling over in his heart, breaking, dancing.

So it was with him as he watched her teeth cut into the turnip. He didn't say anything at all. Nor did she. Shortly afterwards the bell went, and it was only later that she had sent him a note, by devious passage across the classroom, thanking him for the turnip. He had the message in his breast pocket at that moment. It simply said : "The turnip was delicious." And that was all. It wasn't even signed. It was like a message a spy might send across a foreign land, the word "turnip" standing for some weapon of war of inconceivable destructive power which he had been sent to explode. Sometimes Malcolm would take out the note and read it, studying it for hidden meanings, a code of the heart promising love, not realising that there was something rather comic in the words objectively considered. To him, the words were as marvellous as a poem by Keats.

Yet he was beginning to realise that she wasn't as innocent as he had thought. He had once overheard her telling another girl of a book which they were both reading called *No Orchids for Miss Blandish*. He knew by their sniggers that it was indecent, but at the same time she had looked so desirable when she was speaking that he was almost overcome by a wave of love and shame. Nowadays, he had dreams of feeding and protecting her, and imagined himself as some kind of caveman bringing back meat to his mate as she waited for him in the morning of the world, full of leaves and sunlight. But there had been no other sign apart from that message. She still went with Ronny who, to crown everything, was the captain of the school football team, a prefect, tall and elegant, a cosmopolitan being of a kind of French radiance. Indeed, he had been to France with his father.

But there was the note and that was something. He began to think of how she had surged into his life. He had hardly noticed her at the beginning. How strange that was, that she had been on his class as a kind of absence for three months before he noticed her at all. And the incident that had brought her to his notice had happened about a year previously.

It had happened in the class of Mr Moore, a big brutal man of whom everybody was terrified. He taught history and sometimes, if he was in a good mood, he would joke with a ponderous pedantry, but at other times he would fly into the most unpredictable rages, flagellating the desk with a huge ruler that leaned in calmer weather against the wall, distempered in a vague blue. He taught his own registered class religious knowledge, and one sure way of antagonising him was to arrive without a bible : at nine o'clock in the morning he was usually in a vile temper anyway. Looking back now, Malcolm could afford to find this absurd, the uninhibited rages during a period supposedly designed to teach love and humility. But in those days he was simply terrified.

One morning, Ronny had come without his bible and Moore had begun on him, pacing up and down beside him, his hands clasped behind his back, twisting and untwisting, the large blue veins prominent.

"Is there no bible in your home?" he boomed. "Are you a race of heathens? Did you not think of borrowing one from the library?" Foam brimmed at his mouth.

Ronny sat there, smiling insolently but saying nothing.

57

Malcolm tried to bring the image into focus. It was an image of negligence, insouciance, a slim boy eventually standing up in a navy blue blazer, tall and cool and looking a little bit bored. His attitude was so strange in view of the terror that Moore normally inspired that the class sat looking on in petrifaction, and even into Moore's reddening eyes had crept a rather worried, wary, judging look.

He had, of course, belted Ronny but the latter had not turned a hair. It seemed that the incident was over, till the following morning when Ronny arrived again without his bible. Moore had stared at him as if he had seen a ghost, a nemesis, one of the cold uncontrollable parcae of mythology, his ruler held tightly in his hand, his knuckle whitening as the fist closed and unclosed. It was while Moore was gathering his forces for the storm—inside which Ronny remained calm and cool—that Malcolm had seen Ronny turning and smiling briefly at Janet, she smiling back and then lowering her gaze as Moore watched her.

It was then that both Malcolm and Moore realised that Ronny was doing this for her. That day, Ronny was belted again and finally sent out of the room altogether at the bible period. He had achieved a victory over Moore who became more manic than ever and whose hatred of Janet grew to terrifying proportions, so much so that he had once thrown a big green history book at her for some trivial offence. It was as if Moore sensed himself inside a maelstrom of forces that he couldn't control, precisely because they were the forces of life itself. One would sometimes see him looking at the class with a certain puzzlement, his hand clenching and unclenching on the ruler, his moustache twitching. He would stare at Janet for long periods as if she were a cinder which he wished to squeeze in his fist and put out for ever, always trying to catch her out with some date or footnote to mediaeval history, but she was very quiet—stunningly pretty in the morning of her beauty—and her very existence a triumph over force and disorder. But of course he did manage to get her into difficulties, for she wasn't very clever, and finally Ronny had given in, not to save himself but to save her and then Moore was happy again to find the rebel brought to heel, the bible on his desk punctually every morning. Christianity having triumphed once more. Sometimes he would take a walk down the passageway and stand behind Ronny's desk, glancing down at the bible not saying a word but confirming that it was there, that the victory was his, that the Jehovah with the ferrule had established his rule over the swarming devils of darkness.

That was when Malcolm had noticed Janet for the first time, and ever since then he had brooded about her. But there was no way of getting her away from Ronny and his admiration was a hopeless one. Sometimes he thought of fighting Ronny but he knew that he would lose. He would beat him however at schoolwork, because Ronny didn't care. In his negligent way he made his way through school without exertion but without brilliance, quizzical, speaking little, relaxed.

He thought of this too as he sat on the headland watching the ships, and wishing that he were a pilot in a Spitfire, high up in the air, veering and turning and blitzing Moore in vicious acrobatics over the mediaeval history books and the coloured bibles.

THE TOWN HAD a population of about 5,000, though of course the war had diminished it. There was a Town Hall, a library, numerous churches whose congregations streamed to them on Sundays in their rigid black, one cinema, three cafés, two newspaper shops and a variety of other buildings. The town stood by the sea and on certain days one could see the women in blood-coloured gloves gutting the herring and laying them tier on tier in their boxes of ice.

He spent a lot of time in the library. Once he had stayed a whole afternoon and was found there by an emissary sent by Miss Miles. He had completely lost himself in the world of upper-class magazines, leather-covered chairs and newspapers. He would go from paper to paper reading the *Scotsman*, then the *Glasgow Herald,* then the *Express* sadly thinned by the scarcities of war. On Mondays, he mostly read the football reports. This life progressed step in step with the war. One year he would be reading about the African campaign with its thrust and counter-thrust of tanks racing across infinite deserts. How capable Rommel looked, standing in the glare, wearing his goggles, and staring across to the British lines. Another year, it would be Timoshenko standing up in a frozen tank. He liked the library with its smell of varnish and comfortable leather and at times he would stand at the window looking down on the town, a hawk, he liked to imagine, looking down on the world of lesser birds. The novels he borrowed from the library were mostly by P. C. Wren.

Other times he would go and look at the boats which were tied up alongside the quay. He liked to watch the men in their white woollen jerseys and their wellingtons. He liked to see one of them sitting like a cobbler on the deck, mending his nets in a humdrum domestic atmosphere. He liked to watch the seagulls standing precariously on the wooden ledge rimming the stone quay, winking at him with idiotic moronic gaze. He liked the colours, the yellow of the oilskins, the green of the nets, the blue of the water. He liked to see the lanterns on the masts, the orange buoys, the names of the ships picked out in yellow, "Resolute", "Island Queen", and many others. Once or twice he'd been down in the galley of a motor boat with a local boy who was the cook, but he had been put off by the smell. He liked the feeling the boats gave him of another world, a world connected with the vast spaces of the sea, storms, illimitable horizons.

Sometimes he met one of the fishermen from home and talked to him, though he sensed that the fisherman didn't think much of his pale face and scholarly appearance. At the same time he himself compensated for this by imagining that the fisherman looked very clumsy and unsophisticated away from his boat and the sea.

His mother would come up town now and again to do some shopping and he would meet her for lunch; they would go to one of the cafés where he would sit with her in an agony of embarrassment among the pupils, giggling over their ice drinks, she in her black coat and black hat, stiffly seated at the round-topped table with its veined inferior green marble.

"Won't you introduce me to your friends?" she would say, but he would mumble that his friends actually weren't in the café at the time. Who in fact were his friends, the villagers or the town boys?

"Where is the son of the minister you were telling me about?" she would ask, but he was careful to make sure that he never came. How pitiful she looked in this new environment, like a rabbit looking about it, nose nervously twitching.

Once one of his teachers had passed and he had pointed him out. She had said: "Why don't you introduce me?" and then looking at the teacher carefully: "Mrs Mackenzie said he was forty. He can't be more than thirty-five. And he's bald, too. She didn't tell me that."

She was glad of this additional fact: it was worth putting in her bank. Usually after he had had his dinner he would wander round the town and perhaps look at the trailers on the cinema. There was one film that he always remembered. It was called "Wake Island" and was about the war in the Pacific between the Americans and the Japs. It showed a Japanese pilot in black helmet and goggles scowling ferociously behind the controls of a plane and a great area of flame behind him branching out into the Rising Sun. He could imagine his own hands tightening on the controls in the summer light, and the roar of the crowd cheering him on as he swooped out of the sun, guns flaring. Other times there were films of Laurel and Hardy. These he didn't particularly care for. Sometimes he would walk down to the local newspaper offices and say to himself: "If I get a place in the Bursary Competition, I'll have my name in the paper."

When he was younger and before he went to the town school he only went to town once a year. He could still remember the rank foreign scent of the apples, the coolness of ice cream on his teeth, the sound of cinema gunfire in his ears, himself crossing mesas among cactus more alien, more needly than gorse. He even remembered his very first day in the town school, wearing his new brown suit, and being dandled on the knees of a girl on the bus and she saying, "My big man," while her bangles clattered and her cheap perfume was a corrupt aura. He liked the freedom of walking about the town because he didn't feel that anyone was watching him as they would be at home in the village, the worst ones being the religious people. In town he could walk along without having to look over his shoulder. What could he not do if he wished? There were no familiar faces at the windows and no twitchings of curtains.

On wet days he would spend a lot of time wandering through Woolworths, looking for cheap books (such as the *Phantom* and the *Spider*), studying which note books to buy, which pencils to use. All was colourful, but he couldn't afford much. Sometimes he would meet one of the boys from the village during the lunch hour and they would go into a café or down to the boats. Once Dusky had said to him :

"Do you remember the day we had the fight in the school?" The village school. Yes, he remembered.

"I thought you were getting snooty," said Dusky, "just because you were going to the town school. That was the cause of it." He spat expertly on to the pavement. "I thought that right enough."

Actually, Malcolm had thought they were fighting because they had had an argument about an aeroplane which had just flown over them, whether it was a Hurricane or a Spitfire. He remembered the two of them standing by the crumbling wall looking up at the blue hollow shield of the sky and the aeroplane quite low down.

"That was the cause of it," said Dusky. "I wish I had stayed on. I was good at writing," he added. "Here, I'll buy you a lemonade. I wish I'd stayed on all right. Oh, look at that!" whistling after one of the schoolgirls in her uniform of black with yellow stripes. "I bet they're pretty hot," he said, winking at Malcolm.

"I don't know, I suppose so," said Malcolm, and was surprised at his distaste that Dusky should be talking about them in such a familiar way. He was also thinking about that fight and the blood on his nose, all because, as he had thought till now, of an aeroplane. The fight had been a one-sided one : he had lost in a short furious engagement behind the school at four o'clock. The other thing he remembered was bending his face under the water spurting from an old copper tap and later feeling if he had all his teeth intact. As well as that, he could hear again the tongue lashing he had received at home, as if he had been responsible.

Ah, well, it was all over now : he could afford to pity poor Dusky, condemned to servitude in the galley of a fishing boat, and probably putting sugar instead of salt into the men's soup.

[10]

THAT MONDAY EVENING just before he went on the bus he met Sheila standing outside the cinema. She was wearing a yellow coat, her black hair neatly shining, her high cheekbones heavily powdered above the rather too thick lips. She was shorter and squatter than Janet, less fine, her legs stronger and fatter than Janet's: where Janet was air and fire she was earth.

He talked to her, swinging his bag in an embarrassed way.

"Going to the flicks?" he asked.

"What do you think?" she said, half impudently.

When he went to their house she was always quiet, sometimes standing behind him as he played her father at draughts, watching with a kind of contempt the latter's rather neolithic efforts at strategy. When she was in town as now her personality seemed to change. She became more of a flirt, more obvious in her tactics, as if she were imitating the town girls who patrolled the streets at night like destroyers. She had just too much lipstick, too much powder, a caricature of what she considered to be sophisticated.

"Waiting for someone?" he asked casually.

At this she looked meaningful and significant, like an amateurish actress in a B picture, but didn't say anything, wearing her mysterious provocative Hollywood look.

Suddenly he burst out: "If I didn't have to go home we could take a walk in the park."

"Why don't you?" she said again. (Rather French now, with the gamin look and the skin-thin raincoat.)

"I meant the two of us, but I have to go home. I've got a lot of work to do," he muttered.

"You're always working," she said in the same coquettish way. Two town boys walking past whistled in unison. She looked at him, smiling, her glazed handbag in her hand.

At that moment he thought of Janet and she seemed so regal, so imperious, so clear beside Sheila that he felt as if he had been guilty of treachery.

For some reason he felt inclined to explain :

"I'm going in for the Bursary Comp," he said, half proudly.

"What's that?" she asked negligently. "Is it something important?"

"Yes. It's quite important." He had sometimes felt that her mother might have wanted him to take an interest in Sheila.

"It means that I would have more money for university," he said.

"Will you write to me if you get to university?" she asked.

"Yes. What's on at the flicks?"

"Tarzan. And there's Laurel and Hardy."

"Do you like Laurel and Hardy?" he asked, patronisingly watching the yellow bus out of the corner of his eye.

"Yes, I like when they throw the pies at each other." She burst out laughing. "His face. The fat one's face. And the thin one always looks so sad. But I like Tarzan better. There's more adventure."

Malcolm was very conscious of her while she was speaking. Was she really going to the cinema on her own?

A sailor on leave, his blue collar flapping, his idle hands hanging down at his sides, was hovering about, looking up and down the street and pretending to study a shop window which contained men's suits.

For a moment their eyes met and he was startled by the avaricious glitter in hers which slowly dimmed into a dark blankness.

"I'd like to come, but I've got to go home," he said.

"Perhaps some other time," she said, as if speaking with another voice, that of the small-time American actress. "I see your brother at the dances."

"Oh?"

"He's a good dancer. But it's always you who come for the butter."

His face reddened. He glanced at the clock. Soon the bus would be leaving. It would be terrible if he missed it.

"I'll meet you some day," he said, "at the dinner interval."

She smiled again, stroking her hair, standing in front of the Hollywood mirror of the bright day. "If you like," she said.

"And I'll write if I get to university."

The sailor was jingling some coins in his pocket, pretending to examine the film trailer. She smiled at him and the sailor smiled back, then looked out to sea where a ship was lying at anchor in the bay.

Suddenly she half whispered to Malcolm : "Everyone says you're very clever."

He saw the bus moving and turned away. As he leaped on to the step he saw her enter the cinema, the sailor following close behind.

The last thing of all that he saw was the sailor removing his cap as he climbed the steps into the cinema. It was like a man going to church, except that he could see a flash of her short stumpy legs ahead of him.

11

THE GAELIC CLASS was a small one. Janet was in it, himself and two or three others. The Gaelic teacher was a small, spectacled man with a ginger moustache, who would sometimes doze off at the desk. When he did so there was a profound silence in the room. None of the pupils moved, they did not turn a page, they did not read, they did nothing except look at each other or perhaps at a fly buzzing heavily in the window. Suddenly the teacher would wake with a start, his ginger moustache seeming to take on animation, and he'd say: "Well, why aren't you working, eh? Why aren't you working?"

That Monday they were studying a love poem by the Gaelic poet William Ross. Little James was seated at the desk next to Malcolm, like a mouse that had been cornered behind a pile of boxes and stays there petrified and motionless. For some reason the Gaelic teacher had taken a strong dislike to James and would shout at him for the most trivial things. On the other hand, Malcolm was one of his favourites.

"William Ross is the greatest love poet in Gaelic," he said. He turned to James: "Well, why aren't you taking that down? Or are you depending on your memory, eh? Do you think you'll get through your Highers by depending on your memory, eh, by going to sleep in the middle of your lessons?"

His face suddenly flushed with rage as if he had been

insulted, and James immediately began to write in a nervous jerky script (as did all the others): "William Ross is the greatest love poet in the Gaelic language."

They waited. After a long while the teacher continued: "He died of TB. In the old days it was called consumption."

Malcolm was looking at Janet, her dark head bent over her book, and he thought of himself as William Ross being nursed by Janet while he wrote poems to her of astonishing beauty and power. He wrote: "William Ross—consumption"; and after that he wrote: "Keats—consumption, Lawrence—consumption, Robert Louis Stevenson—consumption." Without thinking, he said aloud: "Why do so many poets die of consumption, sir?" The island was full of it.

The teacher looked up and smiled: "That, Malcolm, is an intelligent question. A very intelligent question. It is perfectly true that a lot of poets have died of consumption. Can you think of a reason yourself?"

"Unless it is that they are more sensitive than other people," said Malcolm lamely.

Suddenly James said. "Burns didn't die of consumption," and then retreated into himself as if he had returned from a daring reconnaissance.

"What?" said the teacher. "What did you say? Burns? Yes, true, Burns was a love poet," he admitted grudgingly. "In fact he is said to have influenced Ross. Calder says that. Yes, Calder has a few words on that in his valuable introduction. But then Burns died young too. Though of course it wasn't from consumption."

James looked down at his book like a nun at her rosary.

"Perhaps then we should rephrase the question," said the teacher cheerfully. "Perhaps we should ask: why do so many poets die young, even if they don't die of consumption."

Malcolm suppressed a terrible impulse to laugh but the teacher himself lost interest in his question as if he had heard it somewhere before many, many, years ago and he had answered it once and for all. His eyes began to close and he forced them open.

"William Ross's most important poem is the one to Summer. It begins: 'Oh let us wake joyfully and gladly.' These are the opening lines. And make sure that you know some of these lines for your Highers. Additional marks can be gained by correct quotation; though on the other hand incorrect quotation may lose you marks. I'm tired of telling you that you must be able to quote accurately."

What beautiful lines, thought Malcolm. "Oh let us waken joyfully and gladly. Let us waken joyfully and gladly", and he thought of himself getting up in the morning and walking across cool green linoleum while everyone else in the house was asleep.

He had no fears about his Gaelic. He would pass his Gaelic all right.

After a while the teacher looked up again and said: "There was a love poet in Janet's village. Wasn't there, Janet?" His mouth wreathed itself into the semblance of a smile.

"I think so, sir," said Janet, smiling brightly back.

"Do you know his name, Janet?"

"It was Mackinnon, sir, wasn't it?"

"No, it was MacLennan." His smile remained in spite of the wrong answer. James was watching him and his mouth twisted into a frown. Malcolm wished that she had known the poet's name.

The teacher leaned back in his tall skeletal chair. "Yes,"

he said, "He wrote a lot of love poems. But they were all to his wife." He waited for the laughter to subside and then continued: "He went abroad to Australia or somewhere."

Malcolm was listening, but at the same time an original verse was forming in his mind:

> *The wind moves above the draughtboard.*
> *I see your face beside his dying face.*
> *There are daffodils growing in the garden.*
> *Your face is white as the moon.*

Where had that verse come from? Quite spontaneously it had been forming below the surface of his mind.

He listened again.

"Yes," said the teacher, leaning forward, his hands judiciously clasped. "He has a verse which goes something like this:

> *"Love will not die.*
> *It is like the sun behind clouds.*
> *It is like gold that will not rust.*
> *It is like rock with the sun on it."*

"That is quite beautiful," said Malcolm, blushing as he spoke.

"I'll tell you," said the teacher, becoming more expansive as the end of the period approached, "Janet can bring you the book, Malcolm. I'm sure her parents will have a copy. No harm in breadth of reading. No harm at all. You might get something out of it for the Highers. They might look more favourably on you if you compared the two poets. Can you do that?" he asked Janet.

"I think so, sir," said Janet. "I think I'll get it from home."

71

"Good, good. Now," he said, becoming brisk, "take this down. William Ross, apart from being a great love poet, also wrote a drinking song and a song about the Jacobites." He continued for some time to dictate till the bell rang.

As they were going out, Malcolm said to Janet: "Will you remember to bring the book?"

"Yes," she said, "next time I go home I'll bring it. You're very interested in poetry, aren't you?"

"Yes, I'm pretty interested."

She looked at him in her half mocking way, her books on her arm.

"Yes, I knew you were. I'll see if I can find it. I can't promise, mind, but I'll try."

Suddenly he blustered out: "I suppose you're still going with Ronny?"

"Who told you that?"

"Oh, I know. Everybody knows that."

"Well then, ask no questions, get no lies." And again he hated Ronny, son of a prosperous town lawyer, lots of money, car, good footballer, captain of the school, captain of the football eleven. Their house stood all by itself in great grounds with a curving drive and a garden red with flowers. There was a bell push set in the stone. He knew the house all right but had never been inside it.

She suddenly laughed. "Anyway, we've just proved that poets die young."

She turned away, leaving him with James to whom he said:

"I can't understand why he's after you all the time."

"Can't be helped," said James bitterly. "If it's up to him I won't get my Gaelic in the Bursary Comp."

"But it's not up to him," said Malcolm, watching Janet going away, his heart aching with longing.

"No, perhaps not," said James, his small eyes flashing. He didn't say anything more but walked beside Malcolm along the corridor, the light flashing through a window as they passed. What a beautiful day. What a priceless summer. Framed in the window they saw some boys playing football, and Malcolm's legs seemed to move over grass, great power accelerating through them. And then he thought of Janet again, and the book. But later he felt the real ball at his feet.

"I'll get where I want without him," said James, his veined hands clutching his book. "He doesn't know much anyway." Malcolm was surprised at the bitterness in his voice. He himself could truly say that he had never felt bitterness in his life.

"Yes, isn't that funny," he said, bursting out laughing. "William Ross is the greatest love poet in the Gaelic language, as if that was the Sermon on the Mount. As if that was an important statement."

Below his mind a new verse moved:

> One face dies. The other is alive.
> One has chequered shadows and the other
> moves in the yellow wind ...

12

THINGS WERE CHANGING at Dicky's house. As
his health deteriorated so his mother was beginning to
discourage visitors, except for the minister who was there
more often than the doctor. Malcolm thought sometimes
that it might have been better if he had had brothers or
sisters. Dicky was now in bed all the time in a small room,
the windows of which were often curtained across, his
throat covered by a white bandage. Beside him was a table
on which were tumblers, pills and a bible. In front of him
was an old dresser on which was perched precariously a
green helmet in green netting. Where it had come from
Malcolm couldn't tell. They no longer played draughts. In
the first instance Dicky was too weak to play and in the
second his mother was beginning to think that such acti-
vities were frivolous.

One day Malcolm was sitting by his bedside when the
minister came in, removing his hat and bending as he
crossed the threshold. "Ah, you're Mrs Gordon's boy," said
the minister, looking at him keenly, happy that he had
recognised him.

Malcolm didn't know what to say, so didn't say anything. He wanted to get away but couldn't think of a way
of leaving without embarrassment. He shifted his position
in the chair and looked at Dicky's mother, who was standing in the doorway, smiling sadly at the minister. She was
wearing black and her face was gaunt and lined. Malcolm
thought that she was beginning to dislike him for some

reason : yet he had been the most consistent visitor of anybody.

"And how are we today?" said the minister, gazing benevolently at Dicky whose face was chequered with the sunlight and shade cast on it by a lime-green curtain.

Dicky didn't say anything. On his face there was a slight flush. He was gazing from his bed towards the window and listening to the sounds coming from outside, the mooing of cows, the bark of a dog, the sudden crowing of a cock. The minister, clad in his black coat, leaned forward : "I will read you a passage from the bible." He said this as if he were about to prove a continual expertise in himself. Dicky's mother folded her hands. The minister continued : "For if we haven't the bible, what have we? We are but sinners and there is no grace in us."

He stretched out his hand for the bible on the dresser, changed his mind and took one from his pocket. He read with fine articulation and great style a passage from the Old Testament. The whole room seemed to have become frozen, the human beings in it scarcely breathing and the curtains almost ceasing to sway.

"And it came to pass after these things that God did tempt Abraham, and said unto him, Abraham : and he said, Behold here I am. And he said, Take now thy son, thine only son Isaac, whom thou lovest, and get thee into the land of Moriah; and offer him there for a burnt offering upon one of the mountains which I will tell thee of ..."

In the doorway, Dicky's mother was standing in the attitude of a statue looking down at the floor. Malcolm suddenly thought : she is seeing her son dying, and it became real to him for the first time. And the thought also came to him : if I were seeing my mother or my brother dying what would I feel? And the room became chillier than ever, so that he wanted to be outside where it was hot and where there were flowers growing.

Dicky's eyes were closed. One couldn't make out whether he was listening to the words or whether he was lost in a dream of his own without energy. The green helmet looked moss-coloured in the green light, like some object under-water. The floor was chequered with light and shade like a draughts board.

"Then on the third day Abraham lifted up his eyes and saw the place afar off. And Abraham said unto his young men, Abide ye here with the ass; and I and the lad will go yonder and worship, and come again to you. And Abraham took the wood of the burnt offering, and laid it upon Isaac his son. . ."

The minister's head was bent over the book so that one could see the startlingly live hairs on the back of his neck. His white finger, fat as a worm, touched the page, seem-ing to follow the writing word by word. It all seemed so unreal, like swimming about at the bottom of the sea wearing a diver's helmet. Outside, the grass was growing rich and green and hot. Here on the other hand, there was this droning voice and a woman standing at the door, black and gaunt.

"And Isaac spake unto Abraham his father, and said, My father: and he said, Here am I my son. And he said, Behold the fire and the wood: but where is the lamb for burnt offering?"

The moor aflame, the sun rising like a cock crowing behind a creel, Sheila's lips laughing . . .

"and bound Isaac his son, and laid him on the altar upon the wood. And Abraham stretched forth his hand,

and took the knife to slay his son. And the angel of the Lord called unto him out of heaven . . ."

And Lawton and Gillick and Carter in their strips and white shorts landing like angels on the green sward, the globe at their feet.

"And he said, Lay not thine hand upon the lad, neither do thou anything unto him : for now I know that thou fearest God, seeing thou hast not withheld thy son . . ."

And the lime-green curtains swayed and Malcolm kept his mouth shut lest the germs should enter.

"And Abraham lifted up his eyes, and looked, and behold behind him a ram caught in a thicket by his horns : and Abraham went and took the ram, and offered him up for a burnt offering in the stead of his son . . ."

And the room was so warm and musty and there were Japanese pilots clad in black turning and spinning in the sky, buzzing. And the minister closed the book and stood up and said, "And now let us pray."

And Malcolm found himself kneeling on the floor, his hands propping his chin while he stared at the brown linoleum, scarred with many boots.

". . . once again offer thanks to thee who art our saviour and who gave thy only begotten son that we might be saved by his intercession, that we should not perish but have eternal life. Thou who restored unto Abraham the son of his loins after thou didst command him to sacrifice the fruit of his old age. We come to thee in trembling and in adoration, for your dealings with us are kind beyond our deserving and it is not our part to question that covenant which thou madest with us. Let thy hand stretch over this house and over him who is lying on the bed of sickness and her who keeps the watches of the night. Be thou gracious unto them and make them to know that thou art constantly thinking of them and that our life is not a vain dream but an offering meet for thy receiving."

Shifting a bit, Malcolm looked sideways and noticed for the first time that the bible was lying on top of a Penguin *New Writing*. He smiled to himself very carefully. "And make him to come to thee in love and adoration knowing that thou alone art his true saviour and his true stay and that with thee aie the sweet waters of salvation. Amen."

The minister unclasped his hands. He bent down and said to Dicky, who was breathing with difficulty :

"I hope that you will be better when I come again which, please God, will not be long."

He smiled warmly but Dicky's eyes remained closed. As he got up, Dicky's hands touched the bible accidentally. It was cold though the sun seemed to be illuminating it. The minister went out, talking to Dicky's mother and clasping her hand in his, and Malcolm, with one last look at Dicky, followed him. He said goodbye to Dicky's mother in an embarrassed rush. But she hardly seemed to notice him, so occupied was he with the minister, her cheeks flushing with what might have been pride.

Instead of going round by the gate, Malcolm jumped over the wall, landing in the dry ditch among all the rusty canisters, pieces of wood with nails sticking out of them, bottles flashing in the sun, and made his way home. In a field in the distance a blade flashed like a semaphore. A little dog ran along in front of him, purposefully intent on its business, its eyes shining. He saw a black snail on the road and on the edge a daisy with the yellow sun blazing out of the white. In the sky a lark was singing deliriously and far in the west a crow was sauntering about. The scent of summer growth was in the air, musky and heavy as sleep.

13

H is mother didn't want him to go to the wedding party or réiteach that night. She didn't like him being away from his studies. This, of course, didn't apply to Colin but then he didn't do any studying anyway. Standing at the washing line and taking the pegs out of her mouth she said: "I don't understand why you want to go. You never wanted to go to weddings before."

"I need a break sometime."

"You should have your break when your examinations are over. You'll soon be sitting your bursary and you should be working every night. I don't want you to go the way your father went. He was clever but he wasted it."

Her thin nose interrogated the air.

His father had run away to sea when he was sixteen and had served in ships all over the world from Liverpool to Hong Kong. It was perhaps a myth that he had been clever but it suited her to keep it up.

"And I brought you up to be a cut above these people. Remember, they've never been out of the island, and I have and I've seen the world."

She didn't like him visiting Dicky so much.

"You might get TB," she would say, "and then what would happen to your career? He should be in a sanatorium though I've nothing against the boy. He was always a nice boy."

The sheets hung above her in the breeze like ghosts.

Sometimes she would tell of her time in Yarmouth and

how poor Peggy had pulled the communication cord by mistake and a little railway man with a peaked cap had come into the compartment to investigate and Peggy didn't understand what it was all about and all the other girls had pointed at her and then at their forehead, the strategy being easy to execute as Peggy couldn't speak a word of English.

She was very tough, there was no doubt about it, but Malcolm was determined to go to the wedding party, partly because it was Donny who was marrying and Donny was Dell's brother and he was home on leave from the Navy. He liked Donny and thought he should go to his wedding. So he went.

He combed his hair just like Colin did and put on his blue suit and his blue jersey and his black shoes and walked across in the night with the moon just rising in the sky, thinking of the Vergil on his table, which gave him a slight touch of conscience but surely he couldn't be expected to be working all the time. His mother had probably placed it there quite deliberately : and he didn't like that. But at the same time he could see her point of view too. But he didn't like her attitude to her neighbours. After all, they had been very kind, especially the summer before when he had come home with the two silver cups and all the other prizes he had won. They had been very flattering and the story had gone round that he was one of the most brilliant students the school had ever had : only he knew how wrong this was.

14

HE COULD HEAR the music from the house even before he reached it. He crossed the moonlit plank and walked along the road towards Donny's house. It was eleven o'clock at night and the road was white with light, as were the roofs of the houses, and the smell of the flowers mixed with salt was in his nostrils. He put his hand on the wooden gate, lifting the sneck and remembering to close it behind him. He stood there for a moment listening to the music growing louder. He walked down the earthen path, stepping delicately in his polished shoes, and came round the side of the house, from the windows of which there was no light because of the black-out. He stood there for a moment looking out towards the sea with the moon shining on it in white scrolls and felt a strange melancholy mixed with excitement. The night was as bright as day.

He entered the barn at the side of the house and stood gazing round him into the dancers, who were whirling round in an eightsome reel, emitting sudden shrieks as they did so. For a moment as he stood there he felt like a stranger. The dancers were so involved in their dancing, their faces so flushed and sweating, their concentration so intense that they wouldn't notice him. He remembered the story of William Ross, who had been struck with love by the sight of a girl with golden helmet and ordered hair, gazing back at him out of the dance.

Donny was marrying young Jessie, a buxom girl with big breasts who would make a good mother but had no fire about her at all. He couldn't see either of them and thought they might be in the house. Most of the dancers seemed to be under eighteen and some old and middle-aged people were sitting around watching them.

Tinker was sitting on a bench and said "Oidhche mhath" as he came in. Malcolm said "Good evening" and sat down beside him. A girl's eyes, wide open, rested on him for a moment mindlessly and then were gone as she was carried away shrieking.

"Ah, we can still have a wedding," said Tinker, who was smoking a small stubby pipe, "but it's not so good in time of war."

"No," Malcolm agreed as a red skirt whirled past.

"Not as in the old days," said Tinker reflectively. "We used to have a small réiteach and a big réiteach and a wedding." He paused. "The things we used to do!"

Malcolm gazed down on to Tinker's head, which was bald as a stone and partly corrugated.

"What did you use to do?"

"We painted Hugh's door red," said Tinker, laughing quietly and then coughing because of the smoke. "It was green usually and when he woke up in the morning it was red. I never saw a man so dumbfounded in all my days. He thought he was in the wrong house." Here he began to splutter again. "He kept looking at the door and scratching his head." Tinker took the pipe out of his mouth and jabbed at Malcolm with it. "You see it was green before and then it was red. Hughie was scratching his head and the beauty of it was he didn't like red paint anyway. Not a bit. The things we used to do," he said again. "Do you remember Bellag?" he said screwing up his eyes.

"Yes. She used to stay alone, didn't she?"

"Ay, she's dead now. Well she used to stay in this thatched house. She was mad, you know. She used to go after rats all night. Well, we took a string and a dead rat and we were stroking it up and down the door and she would rush out and we would go round the side of the house and she would look up at the sky with her mouth open ..." He went off into a paroxysm of coughing and laughter. The music stopped and Big Dan was seen with his accordion, one foot resting on an upturned box, his eyes unsmiling and clear.

"They won't get him in the war," said Tinker, clamping his pipe between his teeth.

Sheila waved to Malcolm and he got up excusing himself.

"Where's Dell?" he asked.

"I don't know. He said he was coming but I haven't seen him. He'll come later on."

Squat and dark in her yellow she looked up at him, her wide mouth open in a smile.

"Would you care to dance?" she said, curtseying mockingly and keeping her eyes fixed on him.

The music began again and he put his arm round her, feeling the cloth rustle under his fingers. Looking down he saw that she was wearing black shoes with a pink ribbon on them, and a pleated skirt. She slid closer to him, her eyes closing under the spell of the music. He could feel the rank perfume wafted up from her.

"I wonder where Dell is," he said.

"I don't care," she said almost angrily. "He should have come when he said. He's with your brother most likely."

"Yes."

The Faoilcag drifted past tall as a stork and he waved to her.

"Have you seen Donny?" he asked.

"He's in the house."

"How much leave has he got?" he asked.

She laughed. "What questions. I think he's got two weeks. He'll need them all," she said coarsely. Tinker was watching them with his small beady eyes, pipe clamped between teeth, and thinking probably that the young people nowadays weren't so well behaved as they were in his youth, when green doors were painted red in the middle of the night.

Malcolm suddenly thought : "Why do I always feel as if I'm being watched in this place?"

Seventeen-year-old Donald, who was going to be the captain of the local football team, nodded to him as he swung past, his arm round a red-haired girl, his gipsy cheeks shining.

"When is the food?" said Malcolm, looking down into Sheila's upturned face.

"Whenever you like," she said. His heart began to beat furiously so that for a moment he missed the tempo of the music and had to apologise for his clumsiness.

He thought : "Perhaps I could take her home. On the way there are cornstacks. Suppose we left now."

"Do you want a breath of fresh air?" he asked, controlling his voice.

"Up to you," she said. He held her by the bare arm as they manoeuvred their way through the crowd towards the door. As they stood outside they heard a giggle coming from the side of the house and then Tinker's voice : "They should have shut the door. Don't they remember there's a black-out?"

They stood together watching the sea miles in the distance and the islands, all green in the daytime, now golden. In front of them the cornstacks were all golden too. In the distance he could hear a plover crying and the sound of a river flowing.

He felt the silken rustle of her dress below his hand. Without his thinking his hand slid down her side caressing her back and then her buttocks. She turned in his arms, looking up at him without saying anything. Then her eyes seemed to close. He looked into her half closed eyes and the veined eyelids and at that moment heard a drunken cry:

"What the hell are you doing there?"

It was Dell and he was drunk and beside him was Colin. Dell's collar was open and he was waving a bottle of beer in his hand. Sheila moved away and looked disgustedly into the distance.

"What are you doing?" said Dell. "Eh?" He came closer holding the bottle in his hand. "Think you can do anything, eh? Just because you're a student. Is that right, eh? Well, by God I'm going to teach you." He began to take off his jacket fumblingly, throwing the bottle on to the ground. Colin was still watching, not saying anything.

Malcolm felt suddenly cold. "I'll have to fight him," he thought. So far he hadn't spoken a word.

Dell was struggling with his jacket and shouting: "You won't play for the village, eh? You're too stuck-up, aren't you? You're a student, that's what you are," and he spat on the ground.

He came over and thrust his face into Malcolm's.

"Do you hear me? Are you going to fight? Eh? Are you going to fight? Man to man, eh?" He suddenly pointed to Sheila, swaying on his feet. "That's my girl. You're my girl, aren't you?" She turned away without a word and went inside.

The earth was white with moonlight and Colin was standing there waiting to see what he would do.

"Look," he said to Dell, his voice trembling, "don't touch me again will you?"

Dell began to laugh throwing his head back like a wolf.

"Did you hear that? Don't touch me. Who do you think you are? You're one of the town boys, aren't you? He thinks he's one of the town boys, Colin." He went over to Colin and put his hand on his shoulder. "Colin's my friend, aren't you, Colin. You're not a town boy, are you Colin?" He seemed almost to kiss him, so close did he thrust his face towards him. "Eh? You're my friend. You're my pal."

Malcolm suddenly felt a terrible isolation. His voice rose. "I told you not to touch me."

Dell walked over to him with the deliberation of the drunk and pushed him, catching him off balance. Malcolm fell and got up slowly. He felt a most terrible anger. Dicky, the English teacher, Ronny, his mother, the eternal Latin, all seemed to swim together in his head and he got up ice cold with rage.

"Look," he said speaking very slowly, "I'm giving you your last warning. You push me again and I'll hit you."

Dell looked at him for a long time, swaying on his feet, his disordered collar drifting about his throat. "Good for you," he said at last. "Good for you. If it wasn't for your brother I'd have clobbered you." He came closer, pulling a bottle out of his jacket pocket. "Have a drink? Just for old times' sake, eh? I'd have clobbered you but for Colin." He sat down on the ground and said again: "There's a bottle. Have a drink." He looked towards the house. "Let's get out of here."

They walked together, the three of them, and sat down

in the shadow of a cornstack, the stubble biting into their bottoms.

"Go on, have a drink, student boy."

Malcolm took the bottle and drank. It was very sour stuff and he didn't like it.

"Go on, go on," said Dell, pushing the bottle at him. "It's all right. I'll get another one. To hell with them. You're Colin's brother. I wouldn't fight Colin's brother. You're a good footballer."

As he drank the filthy beer with Dell's arm round his shoulder Malcolm felt at peace for the first time in weeks and months. This was how life should be, sitting against a cornstack drinking beer with Dell and his brother watching him with a new respect.

"Go on. Drink it all up. It's good for you. Good for that brain of yours. Wish I had your brain, eh, Colin, eh? What'll we do, eh? Out on the fishing boat but, student boy here, he'll have a good job. Good luck to him. Good luck to student boy. Take off your cap to student boy here." He stood up waving the bottle in the moonlight and then collapsed against the cornstack, his legs up in the air. He stayed like that for a long time gazing up into the sky.

"Ay, good old townsboy," he muttered. "When they leave us they leave us." In a maudlin voice he continued: "Ay, I remember, do you remember Miss Mowat, eh? Do you remember the time I put the mouse in her desk, do you remember?" He imitated her voice shrilly. "I'll report you to Mr Craig at once. At once, do you hear? Do you hear?" He began to laugh and he couldn't stop and then he wiped his eyes.

"Have another drink. Old times' sake. Go on." Malcolm wiped the mouth of the bottle in the darkness and drank some more, screwing up his eyes and his mouth.

There ensued a companionable silence during which they all looked out to sea and then Dell said: "I wish I was sailing. I wish I could get out of here. To hell with arithmetic. What's the good of it, eh? You tell me, student boy. And history. What good do they do you? That's what I'm asking. Do you know the answer to that?"

After a long time Malcolm said: "No, I don't." He suddenly stood up and did a little dance and shouted, "I like you, Dell. I thought you were going to fight me there. But I like you just the same. I think you're a great man. A great man."

"Have another drink. We're all great men. Colin's a great man too, aren't you, Colin?"

"Right, I'll have another drink. I'll have another drink. Your good health, Dell."

He suddenly had the impulse to put on Dell's jacket for him and struggled with it for a long time while Dell lay against the cornstack, his feet up in the air, waving the bottle above his head and singing.

Finally he finished. "There you are now. You're presentable. The student boy has put on your jacket for you."

"Ay, you're a good sort," said Dell, "but you keep away from Sheila do you hear, do you hear? You've got enough already."

Swaying he got up, staring at the ground for a long time and with great seriousness as he took his bearings. "Come on, let's go to the dance. Let's all go and get some food. Colin, you come here in the middle and we'll go and get some food. My brother's wedding, you know, and he won't be here for long."

Malcolm looked at his flushed face, his high cheekbones, his unfastened collar, his tie screwed half way round his neck and thought: "I love him. We used to build tents together when we were young. He's real. This is real life. This is what life is about." They walked along together in the moonlight, clinging to each other in a wavering chain, Colin in the middle supporting the two of them, Dell and Malcolm making little dancing steps as they approached the door.

15

THAT SUNDAY, MALCOLM met Dell quite by chance when he was out walking on the moor.

"How's the head?" said Dell, grinning and picking up a stone which he threw at a passing seagull.

"Fine," said Malcolm, feeling, just the same, a certain throbbing.

They walked along, hands in pockets. They saw a lark rise soaring out of its nest and found the nest without great difficulty. It had tanned speckled eggs in it and one chick, its red beak wide open. Dell bent down and touched it. The eggs were warm under their hands. They walked on.

As if by an unspoken compact they did not say anything about the incident the previous night.

Soon they came to a river which ran through a gulley; the bed was stony for the water had dried up. The side they were on was higher than the opposite side and they stood there looking down into the river bed. A column of ants was crawling along on the other side.

"Jump?" said Dell, getting to his feet.

Malcolm looked at the distance which had to be traversed. "Pretty wide, isn't it?"

"I've jumped wider than that," said Dell, his hair blowing in the breeze. They stood there for a moment in the silence, nothing breaking it, not even the sound of an insect. A sheep wandering along by itself regarded them briefly and then went back to cropping the grass.

Dell walked back, his boots making an imprint in the dewy earth.

"I'm going to try it," he said stubbornly.

He ran and stopped at the edge. Then he went back again. This time he let himself go, slithered for a moment on the opposite side, digging his boots into the earth, steadied himself, and turned round, grinning and waving.

Malcolm got up, feeling frightened, his mouth dry. If he slid down among all these stones he could injure himself seriously. He looked across the divide to where Dell was grinning back at him, squatting down on the ground, a blade of grass in his mouth. The longer Malcolm looked, the wider the divide became. When he studied the ground it seemed that the land on his own side was greener and smoother whereas on the other side the earth was more trampled and one was more liable to slip. It was also stonier. At that very moment he saw that Dell was removing some of the stones in case Malcolm landed on one of them.

Malcolm had jumped before and he didn't like the sensation of going through the air, holding on to yourself as if part of you were liable to disappear.

To the south was the village where Janet stayed and he could see smoke rising from the houses as he deliberated. He went back slowly, walked up and had a long look and walked back again. Then he ran and stopped at the edge. He couldn't do it. It was impossible. Looking down at the other side he felt nausea and giddiness and his imagination frightened him as he saw himself broken among the stones in the river bed.

He went back again, Dell watching him steadily as he chewed the blades of grass.

He ran and jumped blindly into space and knew that

something had gone wrong. He was going to slip on the other side. He knew this as well as he knew he shouldn't have jumped at all. He wasn't going to gain a foothold. The tackets in his boots weren't holding. He saw the bank spinning in front of him, he saw the large stones circling below him, and he saw Dell's face for a moment, the hands unmoving, the expression ambiguous. Then a hand was held out to him. He held on to the hand. The hand was pulling him, two hands were steadying him. It felt as if Dell was going to slide down with him, the two of them together, and then he was safe. He straightened slowly looking up into Dell's grinning face, and said "Thanks."

"It was nothing," said Dell walking away, he following him. They carried on, coming round in a curve which took them past the river bed. The sun was high in the sky: they jumped peat banks in silence.

"Tell you what," said Dell suddenly, "let's go down to the school."

"It won't be open," said Malcolm.

"No, but we can have a wander round."

"All right."

They walked on, past the standing stones, meeting no one, except that now and then a bird would fly up in front of them. They descended from the crest of the hill to the back of the school, which was made of old stone, scarred and weatherbeaten. They jumped the wall at the back and landed inside, just behind the privies. They went in. The gutters were urine-stained and there was writing on the wall.

"Merry Christmas to all our readers," said Dell. Pieces of old newspaper were strewn on the floor.

They left the privy and looked in through the window at a classroom. It was much smaller than the ones in the secondary school, dimmer, more cramped. The desks, too, looked small and cramped and old, unlike the yellow ones in the secondary school. A large dim globe stood on a table.

Malcolm had the oddest sensation of returning to a place which he had known but which had at the same time diminished. He remembered writing laboriously on his slate in wintertime with a scratching slate pencil : he could almost feel himself at one of these desks in his woollen shorts. Dell was making faces into the empty room. Strange how small everything had become, as if more suited to dwarfs than to human beings. A lady in a helmet of grey hair like a maenad seemed to move pleadingly towards him. He felt slightly sad thinking of the stained copper taps and his own head inverted below them, the privy with its stained aged stone, the classroom with its faded map of Europe, the seats with the names carved on them, the large lady with the huge bosom, the primary colours that warmed the day.

He didn't speak much for the rest of their walk.

16

M r C o l l i n s s t r o d e into the room, the book open in his hand, the red forelock of hair falling about his face.

"Will you please read, Miriam," he said without looking up.

Miriam obediently began to read :

"i, sequere Italiam ventis; pete regna per undas. Spero equidem mediis, si quid pia numina possunt, supplicia hausurum scopulis, et nomine Dido saepe vocaturum."

"Now, translate please," said Mr Collins, "let me hear you translate." He perched on the window ledge, a bird about to take off.

"Go seek Italy," Miriam began, looking down at the book over her white formal collar.

"No, no. Better would be 'Go look for Italy'. Use 'seek' for *pete."*

Miriam began again. "Go look for Italy . . ." She came to a halt. Collins looked up. "Well, well, have you stopped, girl? *Ventis, ventis."*

Miriam didn't know what to say. She looked down at her book. Malcolm looked at her, not having noticed her much before. Strange how he hadn't known her father was dead.

"Ventis, ventis," said Collins again, pleading with his hands. "Malcolm, what does *ventis* mean here?"

"Before the winds," said Malcolm.

"Good, excellent, quite right. 'Before the winds.' An idiomatic use. Pray continue, Miriam."

She began again. "Go look for Italy before the winds, seek kingdoms through the sea."

"Better would be 'seek your kingdom over the sea'," said Collins. "Better, I think, the singular in this instance."

He waited. She continued. "I indeed hope," she said, knitting her brows.

"Not 'hope'. Better would be, 'I do indeed foresee', if *pia*—now what would *pia* mean there? Ronny, what would *pia* mean there?"

Ronny looked up briefly from his corner seat, his mouth twitching.

"Dutiful, isn't it?"

"Yes, but I think a better word would be ... James, what would you say?"

"Gentle, sir."

"Good, good, James, excellent. Good indeed. 'If tender heaven has any power, that you shall suffer punishment on the rocks and often call on Dido's name.' " Like a litany he began to chant, *"Haurio, hausi, haustum, haurire*—to draw, drink, drain the cup of. Literally, drain the cup of punishments on the rocks."

He continued impatiently :

"sequar atris ignibus absens: et cum frigida mors anima seduxerit artus omnibus umbra locis adero. dabis, improbe, poenas: audiam, et haec manes veniet mihi fama sub imos.

" 'I shall pursue thee, though absent, with fires of hell.' No, that's ambiguous. Better would be 'I, absent, shall pursue thee with fires of hell and when icy death shall sever soul and body' (*artus* of course means 'limbs' but I think we would be justified in saying 'body'), 'my ghost shall haunt thee everywhere. Wretch, thou shalt suffer retribution. I shall hear it and the news shall reach me amid the shades below.' "

Malcolm heard the echoing words. "And the news shall reach me amid the shades below."

Collins looked up and added briefly. "*Fama* of course can mean 'rumour' but here I think we might use the more common word 'news'. Come now, Malcolm, let us move on to line 393. Begin at *At pius Aeneas* ... Construe." His beaked head with the red hair turned towards Malcolm. "*At pius Aeneas, quamguam lenire dolentem* ..."

Malcolm began, "But pious Aeneas, though he longs to calm his pain by consolation and avert her sorrow by words ..."

" 'Dispel', Malcolm. 'Dispel' is better than 'avert'. Much better. In this instance."

Malcolm continued, "sighing deeply and moved in soul by strong love obeys the orders of the gods and returns to the fleet."

He stopped.

"Why have you stopped reading, Malcolm? Have you not prepared it?"

"No, sir."

"Do you mean that you have or have not prepared it? Which? Or is there some other reason? We know of the perpetual weddings in your area"—the class giggled—"and the high incidence of fertility. Eh? Have you or have you not prepared it?"

"That wasn't why I stopped, sir."

"Oh? Some other reason? Some abstruse reason? Please let us all into the secret."

Mr Collins was looking up into the light, his beaked prow of a nose questing, the eyes quick below the brows.

"I don't know, sir. I was thinking."

"Thinking of what?"

"Oh, it's nothing, sir. Shall I go on?"

"No, I wish to hear what you were thinking. In fact I'm sure that all of us are waiting with bated IQs to hear what you were thinking. Aren't we?" He twinkled at the class.

They all murmured appropriately. *Gravitas* had for the moment given way to playfulness: the senator was relaxing.

"It's just, sir, that I thought of his leaving her and then Vergil calling him *pius*."

"Ah, but Malcolm, *pius* doesn't meant 'pious'. We mustn't say that Aeneas was Free Church, must we?"

There was a roar of laughter from the class. Even Miriam smiled faintly above her white collar.

"No, sir, I mean the dutiful part. I meant that Dido was in love with him and then he left her so coldly and then the poet writes *pius*. It's something in the poetry."

"Poetry?" said Collins. "What are you saying about the poetry? Come on, come on. After all Vergil is supposed to be second only to Homer, at least in the civilised parts of the world. But perhaps the news hasn't reached us here amid the shades below." He laughed briefly and the class smiled again.

"I don't know, sir," Malcolm pursued doggedly. "I just feel the poetry becoming cold after she says, 'The news shall reach me amid the shades below'." Why did that line make him shiver almost uncontrollably, that vengefulness, that remorseless love?

Collins looked at him for a long time and then his voice softened.

"What do the rest of you think?" he asked, looking keenly round the class. "Ronny? Have your romantic attachments allowed you to pass judgement on Vergil?"

"On this love affair, sir?"

"Yes, Ronny, if you would bend your sardonic mind towards it. For a moment."

"Yes, sir," said Ronny grinning. "I would say that the whole thing is a bit exaggerated."

"Meaning?"

"Meaning too romantic, sir."

"I see. As we all know, however, that the word romantic has a number of meanings, might you elaborate a bit more?"

"Yes sir. I was just thinking . . ." and then he stopped in midflight, looking at Malcolm, as if some idea had come into his mind. Then he started again.

"I was just thinking, sir, that the ideas presented—I mean those of duty and love, which I take to be the two main ones—are shown rather naively."

"We're listening. Pray continue."

"I mean, sir, that when the gods speak to him and tell him directly that he should go, it seems to me to make the contrast too deliberate."

"You mean as distinct from inner conscience, I suppose."

"Yes, sir."

Collins was no fool : sharp as a needle in fact.

"Malcolm," he said.

"If I may say so, sir, I think that is nonsense. Our conscience is equivalent to their gods. The point is that he led Dido to believe that he was in love with her and then left her and then congratulated himself on the fact."

"It doesn't say that he congratulated himself on the fact," said Ronny quickly.

"No, he doesn't say it. The verse says it. Don't you see? There is the poetry of the passion and then there is the poetry when Aeneas speaks. Which of them is the better? That is the question."

"It is not a football game with one side winning and the other losing," Collins interposed, looking birdlike from Ronny to Malcolm and then letting his eyes rest for a moment on Janet.

"Oh, I don't agree, sir," said Malcolm "The verse tells one. The one who is on the side of life is shown in the verse . . ."

"I don't understand that," said Miriam, "surely it's a question of conscience. I don't know what Malcolm is saying but I think he is right just the same. Aeneas wasn't loyal. He couldn't have loved Dido."

She flushed quickly and looked down at her book. Bred on Annie S. Swan. The squire leaves the girl in the lurch even though she's a queen. She sat upright in her chair looking down at her folded hands.

"James?"

"I am on the side of Aeneas, sir. He had his duty to do. The race is more important than the individual."

"Fascist," said Malcolm suddenly. "What do you think we're fighting for. Isn't that what Hitler says, that the race is more important than the individual?"

There was silence. Collins looked uncomfortable for the first time and his expression became more serious.

"Malcolm, we musn't have you saying things like that."

"I'm sorry, sir, I was referring to the ideas. I didn't mean that he personally was a Fascist."

"I accept the apology and I can see your philosophical point. Do you agree, Ronny? Rome was more important than the individual woman. That is your point, isn't it, James?"

"Yes," said Ronny, "I do agree on the whole."

From the back Neil spoke. "I was wondering, sir, whether there was a race element involved here. Did the

Romans consider themselves superior to the Africans? I mean, Aeneas, wouldn't he for instance consider an African queen inferior? Or am I wrong?"

"A very good point, Neil, a very good point indeed. I think you may have something there. Dido was coloured of course. Line 362 on." Rapidly he turned to the line knowing the book backwards, forwards, inside out. "Here it is. 'While yet she spoke these words she looks on him in scowling anger rolling to and fro her eyes.' " He emphasised the last words. "I think that is what Negroes do. As witness Othello. Have you read *Othello*, Malcolm?"

"No, sir, but I think these arguments are wrong. Aeneas was Trojan anyway. And furthermore I would like to ask what kind of Rome would be founded by an Aeneas who could do that kind of thing?"

Collins rubbed his hands with delight and said: "You're all really excelling yourselves today. Really excelling yourselves. So we arrive at the moral question, the moral origins. Was Rome the kind of place that was corrupted from the beginning? An interesting idea. Very interesting indeed."

"Surely that's rather far-fetched, sir," said Ronny. "The point is that he had to leave because his duty called him. He had to do something. In a way he sacrificed himself as well."

It was strange to hear Ronny arguing for this side, thought Malcolm, before bursting out:

"Sacrificing himself? How did he sacrifice himself? Read the poetry. It's smug. He's smug. He doesn't care. Setting off for another land over the bodies of those he's left behind." A thought seemed to strike him and he added: "Do you know what it is like to be burned?"

"Do you?" said Ronny amusedly.

Malcolm glanced for a moment at Janet.

"No," he said at last. "But I know that it must be painful."

"That is why Carthage failed and Rome didn't," said Neil quietly. "I mean that people indulged themselves in this way. They burned themselves for love. That is not the behaviour of responsible people."

"I suppose it is better that they should burn other people. Like the Nazis," said Malcolm fiercely.

Collins looked at Neil for a moment with a certain sadness and then said :

"Miriam, I believe you were going to say something?"

"Yes, sir. All these arguments are very highfalutin, but the basic fact is that she had thought Aeneas was in love with her and he left her. Then she burned herself. And he slunk away. That's all."

"I agree with Miriam, sir," said Malcolm. "His responsibility was to the individual, not to Rome."

"Janet?"

"I agree with Ronny, sir. She shouldn't have burnt herself."

"Of course," said Collins, "we don't find young women burning themselves now, but perhaps that's because they're not passionate enough."

"He wasn't to know that she was going to burn herself," said Ronny, squinting thoughtfully through the hot sunshine and stretching his legs out.

"No, that's true. But what if he had known?"

"I think he should still have gone. One can't go through life frightened that people will burn themselves on one's behalf. That wouldn't be rational."

"Exactly," said Malcolm, "life isn't rational. That's the

whole point. The Romans tried to make life rational but they didn't succeed."

"They succeeded for a good number of years, if I remember rightly," said Ronny with a laugh.

"They were beaten by the irrational in the end."

"Meaning?"

"Meaning the Goths."

Ronny smiled thinly.

"Ah, well," said Collins quickly, "this is all very interesting but it won't get us through the Highers all the same. Eh?"

"May I ask, sir, which side are you on yourself?" said Ronny humbly.

"Which side am I on? Well, Malcolm seems to find that line very striking, the line where Dido says that she will hear the news amid the shades. I find Aeneas' lines also striking. I quote :

" 'But the gentle Aeneas though he longs to calm her pain by consolation and dispel her sorrow by persuasion sighing deeply and moved in soul by her strong affection— still he obeys the orders of the gods and returns to the fleet.'

"I find these lines very moving I must confess. They are so typically Roman."

17

As THEY WERE all going out the door at the end of the period Janet handed him a book.

"What's that?" he asked, having forgotten for the moment.

"It's the Gaelic poetry book," she said.

Ronny was looking at them quizzically and Janet was looking at Ronny strangely. It was such an odd look that Malcolm was for a moment startled out of his pleasure at receiving the book and the fact that she had remembered at all. He knew by his interception of that look that there was something inconceivably intricate between Ronny and Janet. In the sunlight Ronny looked so handsome and gay, so insouciant, so careless, so negligent, the eyes quizzical, the mouth slightly mocking, the pose that of a kind of Byron. And Janet with her tanned face, a kind of Dido? And then Ronny was gone and where he had been was a shadow moving on. *The news will come to me amid the shades.*

"Was it easy for you to get?" he asked.

"Yes. There was one in the house but I didn't know. And I never read it."

"Thank you very much for bringing it. I wondered if you'd remember. You only go home at weekends, don't you?"

"Yes."

"What's the Hostel like?"

"All right."

"Do you get out much at nights?"

"At nights." She looked at him in a startled way. "No, not really."

"I thought . . ."

"What did you think?"

"Nothing. It's all right. It doesn't matter." He had thought she would be going with Ronny.

"What does your father do?"

"My father? Oh he's a painter. Paints houses, not pictures. We are quite poor."

Curious, this way she had of making his heart turn over when he looked at her. It was something innocent, something casual. He knew she wasn't intellectual. It was the careless way in which she carried her beauty, as if she were no one special.

"Well," she said, "that's the book." It was as if she were going to say something else and decided against it.

He didn't want to leave her.

"Will you go to university, do you think?" he asked.

"I don't know. I may not be good enough. I may not get enough Highers . . ."

"Yes, well thank you for the book . . ." Then casually, half moving away, "I don't suppose you'd like to come to the cinema with me some night?"

She looked at him for a moment and then said biting her lip:

"I don't know. I suppose it could be managed. I don't know."

It could be managed. His heart leaped with joy. "When?" he said.

"I don't know yet. I'll let you know."

She left and he watched her going. Then he rushed off

to the next class all on fire. He would take her to the pictures after all, he would defeat Ronny. She turned the corner in her navy pinafore with the yellow belt.

Let us welcome the morning joyfully and gladly.
Let us welcome the morning.

18

THERE WAS AN attic in the house in which was a window from which Malcolm could see the whole village as if in a panorama. All the fields, all the people working in them, the haystacks, the winding river, the fences, the houses, all these could be seen from the window. Often he would climb up to the attic partly to be private, partly to feel like a hawk gazing over its territory. On hot summer days his nose would twitch with the smell of tar from the roofs of the houses, the rank smell of flowers, the salt of the sea blown in by a breeze.

Years before he had found old books in the attic, for example, a series of *Chambers's Journals* printed at Edinburgh in double columns. He had read a lot of the articles. He had also found on old green encyclopaedia. There were rafters from which he could swing and over which he could turn somersaults. In one corner of the attic there was an old box full of old newspapers, old exercise books and old catalogues from J. D. Williams. Sometimes on hot days he would lie on the floor with an old pillow at his head, his legs crossed, looking up at the roof and wishing that there was a window directly above him so that he could look up into the sky. In this confused summer he was going up into the attic more and more. To save appearances he would take Latin books up with him but as often as not he didn't read them. On this particular day he had, as well as his Latin books, the Gaelic book of poetry he had got from Janet and the book with the Auden poem in it.

He looked out of the window for a while but there was nothing much to be seen. The sun was blazing down, the sea was calm, the corn was unruffled by any breeze. There didn't seem to be anyone working anywhere. Now and again he could see Mrs Grant throwing a basin of water on to the grass. The water was almost invisible against the crystal light.

He picked up the Gaelic book and read some of the poems. They seemed to be poems of successful love. The poet's wife had died and he himself had gone overseas to Australia, an alien country "far from the tall mountains and rivers". The poet recalled the village in which he had lived for so many years before his wife's death. He was wishing he might be buried in that village cemetery instead of in hard, dry, strange Australia. He clearly had loved his wife a great deal: he spoke of their children, of whom there were three, and how they were growing up in a strange land "where they never heard the sound of Gaelic". He wrote of how he and his wife had met in their youth and how they had set up house together and he mentioned the neighbours by name and said that he would never see them again. He wrote of his house in the village becoming overgrown with thistles since no one lived there now. He described his days as a sailor with the moon shining above him as he was perched in the crow's nest dreaming of home.

The poems appealed to Malcolm in a primitive direct way because of the Gaelic language in which they were written and he responded more to the pathos and to the music than to the quality of the poetry. Even after one reading he could remember snatches of the poetry which

penetrated his conciousness without any real attempt to
memorise them. The images were few: everything
depended on the music Malcolm himself was transported
to Australia and to exile. The concept of exile had a great
effect on him: in fact it frightened him a little. It was as
if the exile to Australia represented other kinds of exile not
necessarily geographical. A curious unease grew in him as
he read the poems and he couldn't place its source. The
alienness of the landscape seemed to personify some kind
of exile in himself, the feeling of being between two worlds.
It disturbed him and he was irritated that he couldn't place
it. It wasn't that he felt apart from the landscape that he
could see in front of him: it was his home. It was a natural
frame to his life. The people out there were his neighbours.
He knew them all intimately. They seemed to triumph with
him in his achievement: they seemed to praise him for
what he had accomplished. And yet there were uneasinesses.

For instance, in the war there were one or two naval
officers in the village. When they came on leave they were
always friendly to the ratings and acted with them as they
had always done. But the ratings thought of them as
slightly different just the same. And yet the officers couldn't
have been nicer. They weren't really all that high up anyway—just sub-lieutenants. It was this kind of uneasiness
which permeated his mind as he brooded on the idea of
exile. The fact was that sometimes, though he felt anonymous in the town, he also felt a strain. Things were
expected of him. If he faltered, then he would be finished:
he would fall down into their loving pity.

A curious situation had developed which showed this
strain quite clearly. There was one house in the village
which he used to visit in order to listen to the radio. The
man in this house was an ex-sailor who had lived with

his one sister for a number of years. He had left school at fourteen. He was bluff, red-faced, teasing and difficult. He was continually asking Malcolm questions. In those minutes before Big Ben tolled and the news began he would say to him, "Can you tell me how many herring there are in a cran?" or, "What's the Gaelic for an Indian summer?" And his face would appear oily and genial above the moustache.

Malcolm was jolted out of the neat rigours of geometry into this world of miscellaneous knowledge which to him didn't seem so important but to his host was an infallible method of testing a man's intellectual worth. If he didn't know the Gaelic for an Indian summer he was labelled for life. 'Ah, he's clever enough in the books but he didn't know the Gaelic for an Indian summer. What are they teaching them at that school that they've never heard of Indian summers there?'

Sometimes other people would say: "I was good at arithmetic when I was at school but I couldn't stay because I had to go out to work. It's different for you nowadays."

He felt these remarks increasingly as a burden. And sometimes too he began to feel guilty. Was he himself, after all, one of the lucky ones? What about all those poor submerged people all down the centuries—not just his own father and grandfather—but those millions since the history of the world began—had they all lived and died in order that he might write M.A. after his name? It is true that very often he didn't think as consciously as this, if ever, but at the same time uneasinesses were preying on his mind, eating away like a river niggling at its banks.

Yet, of course, the village was not a place of sadness: it was in fact a very happy place. All sorts of songs were written and sung, poking good humoured fun at people, or telling comic stories like, for instance, the one about the man who had bought a cow and on the way home with her had sold her to someone else along the road at a profit. The villagers admired this enterprise but thought it funny.

He picked up the other book, with the Auden poem, gently, frightened in case there were TB germs. It was the first time he had ever borrowed a book from Dicky since he had got TB and he was afraid. Everyone knew what TB was like and what it could do to one, and there was no cure for it, either. He felt the book surrounded by a screen of germs, all hostile, ready to spring up at him into the air, to go straight down his throat and destroy him in obscure anonymous battles.

He opened the window as far as it could go and leaned out, holding the book before him in the blaze of sunshine, imagining that the heat of the sun would destroy the germs. As he was holding the book out he could see his mother below, stretching up to place some washing on the line, watched quizzically by one immobile cow. Her meagre body arched upwards, the slightly rebellious blue and white clothes curving from their geometrical lines. Between her teeth were a clutch of pegs. One by one she took the pegs from her mouth and pegged the clothes to the line firmly. It was strange to be looking down at her like this without her knowing that she was being seen. In some curious way it made her seem like an object, or an animal moving with a purpose of its own but an alien one. The pegging of the clothes on the line appeared for a moment like the purposeful activity of an animal, say, building its nest or fortifying its lair, and this was all the more appropriate as a paradigm since he couldn't see her face, only her back and her hands grained by innumerable washings, red as the claws of a crab. Her hands didn't seem to belong to anyone he knew as they busied themselves with the pegs. Her head, seen from an unfamiliar angle with the coiled greying hair, also seemed not to belong to her. But what intrigued him was the curiously remote way in which he saw her and the curiously remote, purposeful way in which she did things in that silence. It was like watching a scientific experiment.

Where was Janet just now? he wondered. Unnerved by the sensation of dizziness that overwhelmed him when he thought of her, he almost dropped the book on to his mother's coiled head. He thought of how her bare legs looked when he saw her standing by the dappled wall that bounded the school. Then a strange sensation came to him. It was as if the school changed to his village school and she was sitting in one of the cramped seats he had seen when he was with Dell, looking through the window. She was looking out at him almost sadly, as if he had put her there and she couldn't get out. Her legs were turning dark and hairy and when he looked at her face it wasn't Janet at all, it was Sheila, and she was looking down at the floor which had turned into a draughtsboard.

He turned his eyes back to the book, holding it slightly away from him and repeating some of the verses to himself:

Easily, my dear, you move, easily your head
And easily as through the leaves of a photograph album
     I'm led
Through the night's delights and the day's impressions,
Pass the tall tenements and the trees in the wood;
Though sombre the sixteen skies of Europe
     And the Danube flood.

(The sixteen skies of Europe. What did that mean?)

*

Summoned by such a music from our time,
Such images to audience come
As vanity cannot dispel nor bless:
Hunger and love in their variations
Grouped invalids watching the flight of the birds
*   And single assassins.*

*

Certain it became while we were still incomplete
There were certain prizes for which we would never
*   compete;*
A choice was killed by every childish illness,
The boiling tears among the hothouse plants,
The rigid promise fractured in the garden,
*   And the long aunts.*

And every day there bolted from the field
Desires to which we could not yield;
Fewer and clearer grew the plans,
Schemes for a life and sketches for a hatred,
And early among my interesting scrawls
*   Appeared your portrait.*

*

Be deaf too, standing uncertain now,
A pine tree shadow across your brow,
To what I hear and wish I did not;
The voice of love saying, lightly, brightly—
'Be Lubbe, Be Hitler, but be my good
*   Daily, nightly.'*

Who was Lubbe anyway? He thought about the argument in class and himself accusing James of being a Fascist. The idea of saying to James: "Be Lubbe, be Hitler, but be my good, daily, nightly," made him laugh out loud but there was no one to hear him. He practically rolled out of the window thinking of saying to little James: "Be Lubbe, be Hitler, but be my good, daily, nightly."

But after he had laughed he thought of how this poem must have been written about Janet. For the line "A pine tree shadow across your brow" seemed to represent exactly his image of her. He thought of the wall again and the shadow falling across her brow and himself and Neil and James in their flannels surrounding her like a court. The world of the school magazine, the last year when they were being treated as adults for the first time :

> *The power that corrupts, that power to excess*
> *The beautiful quite naturally possess:*
> *To them the fathers and the children turn:*
> *And all who long for their destruction,*
> *The arrogant and self-insulted, wait*
> > *The looked instruction.*

The book of Gaelic poems fell to the floor and he didn't bend to pick it up. He forgot for a moment the screen of germs which his imagination had previously pictured by demoniac summons and stared down at the verse as if in a trance. He moved to the second last verse :

> *Shall idleness ring then your eyes like the pest?*
> *O will you unnoticed and mildly like the rest,*
> *Will you join the lost in their sneering circles,*
> *Forfeit the beautiful interest and fall*
> *Where the engaging face is the face of the betrayer,*
> > *And the pang is all?*

What did it all mean? He couldn't understand it fully but he felt that there was some important meaning there. He fell into a dream of what it was all about while the Latin books lay beside him unread, neglected, and from below he could hear the kettle boiling for the tea.

19

O N E D A Y H E met Miriam by chance down town during the dinner break and he went up to her on impulse.

"I'm sorry," he said, "about the In Memoriams."

"Oh that's all right," she muttered. She was wearing a white blouse and a white pleated skirt and carrying a book under her arm.

"I didn't know about your . . ." He became confused and couldn't continue. They stood together by the sea wall watching a fisherman patiently mending a net.

He continued: "I don't suppose you . . ."

To his surprise she was able to talk quite calmly about the whole business.

"He had cancer," she said. "At least that's what the doctor said."

"Was he in much pain?"

"Yes. It went to his kidneys at first. Then they cut one of them off. Then it went to his arm. They amputated it. Then it went to his spine and that was the end." She stopped and then added: "At the end he said he had lost his faith."

Malcolm was surprised at the way she said this. Casually he said:

"You believe in God then?"

She had been staring down at the fisherman sitting with the brown net in front of him on the deck and holding the mending needle between his teeth while he picked the net up in folds, and she turned round and said:

"Of course. Don't you?"

Malcolm didn't say anything.

"I mean," she added, "how else can you account for things? The sea the sky the stars . . ."

What nonsense it all was. All these people talking about the stars and beautiful sunsets when they had never stopped to look at one in their lives. What was so beautiful about a sunset anyway?

"Do you read the bible a lot then?" he asked.

"Yes, I'm not like some," she said in a flash of what might have been malice.

"Who are you thinking of?" he inquired vaguely.

"Well, there are some of the girls who just read the *Red Star*. I mean in the Hostel."

He wondered if she meant Janet. A cormorant dived into the water in front of him and he watched it while out of the corner of his eye he could see her hand resting gently on the wall all in shadow.

"Such nonsense," she continued. "It shouldn't be allowed. I mean there was a story in one of them. It was about this girl stabbing another one with a pair of scissors just because she was in love with the same man. I was horrified."

"Did you see your father when he was dead?" he asked without thinking, because he was interested. What happened to the dead? What did they look like? Did they look as they did when they were alive? Could one see any sign in them that they had once been alive?

"Yes, I did," she answered. "He hadn't changed at all. He looked just the same except that he was more peaceful. You know, when he was delirious, he was asking for his mother. I could hear him shouting 'Mother'."

Malcolm turned on her with amazement, shocked to the core, imagining this man lying on his bed and in the middle of the night calling on his long dead mother. There was something appalling about it.

"What a terrible thing," he said and was astonished to see a tear trembling delicately below her eye. He watched it trembling, then rounding to a perfect circle and falling down her face and sparkling a little in the sun. It was such a dear marvellous thing. He had never seen such a tear before, such a perfect round tear.

She turned away briefly looking back at the town. He followed her gaze to the picture house where it stood with its doors wide open and the trailers in their frames. And he thought, perhaps I'll be able to take Janet there soon, and as he thought of this the grief which he had just felt turned to inconceivable joy as deep as tears.

Her face turned to him again and this time it was clear and tearless.

"I wonder how many nets they have to mend in a year," he said, looking down at the fisherman in his white thigh-length wellingtons and his blue jersey.

"I suppose they tear a lot," she said.

"Yes, I suppose so. I wonder if he's content. All he has to do is to go out in his ship and then when he's got enough fish he's content."

"I suppose so."

As they were standing by the wall James came along and Miriam said: "Here he is himself." And he knew from the tone of her voice that she didn't like James. James hadn't noticed them. He was walking along head bent to the ground as if studying some secret script or as if looking for lost examination marks, so humble that he seemed to be uncertain of the very air he breathed. Sometimes Malcolm despised him. His hands were clasped behind his back.

Suddenly he noticed them and his eyes lit up.

"Hullo," he said, his eyes becoming wary again. "I meant to ask you something, Malcolm. I wonder if you could tell me. That history paper in the Bursary Comp. Do you know if there's anything about the nineteenth century?"

"Can't tell you," said Malcolm, "haven't seen one yet."

"I've seen all the others," said James moodily, "but not a history one. The others aren't too bad."

"Never mind," said Malcolm, "we'll go into it blind. I'm sure you'll win a bursary anyway." But he didn't really believe this as he didn't think James was very clever. How could a person as mouselike as that be clever?

James blushed, looking sideways at Miriam: "Oh I don't know. I don't think I've got a chance."

"If you swot hard enough," said Miriam staring hard at him.

Suddenly · James said, "I wanted to tell you something."

"What is it?"

James stopped and looked uneasily at Miriam as if he didn't want to speak in front of her.

Realising this she said: "Well, I suppose I'd better be going. And the best of luck with the nineteenth century."

"What's wrong with her anyway?" said James as they watched her crossing the road in her white dress.

"Oh, her father's dead. Perhaps it's that."

"Perhaps."

"What were you going to tell me?" said Malcolm.

"It was just—well, I don't know whether I should tell you—but you should watch out for Ronny Black."

"What do you mean?"

"I don't think he likes you," said James triumphantly. "I think he will try and do you down."

"What makes you think that?"

"He's a bad one," said James. "Do you know what he told me once?" He settled himself against the wall. "He told me once that he had been sitting in his room late at night and he was terribly bored and he thought he'd pick up the phone and ring up Collins. So he picked up the phone and when Collins answered he said: 'How's old Horace today?' and then he repeated that poem, you know the one we had to learn in the English class. 'They told me, Heraclitus, they told me you were dead'."

"And what did old Collins say?" said Malcolm in an amused tone, screwing his eyes against the hard light.

"Oh, he nearly went off his head but he didn't know it was Ronny. Ronny can disguise his voice, you know, he can mimic people. Another thing he told me was that sometimes late at night he would walk along the road and kick at the shop windows and he wouldn't look up to see if there was a policeman there until after he'd finished. It's a kind of dare, he said. Do you believe he would do that, Malcolm?" said James earnestly, looking very much the scholar.

"Oh, he may be pulling your leg."

"I don't know," said James. "Why should he have picked on me? He's the son of a lawyer, you know," he added, "and he can drive, though he's not allowed to go out by himself. He told me he had once driven through our village in his car and he thought it was like an African kraal. He doesn't know what the people are like," said James almost stuttering with indignation.

"Still that was a rotten thing to do to Collins," said Malcolm, "he's not a bad teacher."

"Yes, he's quite good, isn't he? And, another thing, he told me that he took Janet up to the house some nights and he gave her some sherry and they played records. But she didn't know any jazz. All she knew were some old Gaelic records—78s."

He was squinting humbly at Malcolm through the light. Surely he didn't know what pain he was causing. Malcolm imagined Ronny and Janet sitting on the rug in front of the fire in the lawyer's huge house with the records playing and the shadow of the firelight moving over her face and Ronny bending towards her.

Keeping his face as expressionless as he could make it he said: "Is that so?"

"Yes, that's what he said," said James in a disappointed voice. "He told me she used to read *Red Star* and he would read it over with her and he'd never read such junk in his life. But she used to lap it up."

So Miriam was right. But what difference did it make? Reading Karl Marx, reading the *Red Star*, what difference did it make? Was it not better to keep herself beautiful than to think herself into wrinkles?

The fisherman was still mending his net with intent patience.

"So you think he dislikes me?" he said to James.

"Yes, but then he dislikes everybody. And you don't know anything about the history paper? I'd like to know. It's best to know about these questions."

"Why?"

"Why?" James repeated in a perplexed voice. "What do you mean 'why'? If we know the kind of thing they usually ask, then we can prepare for it. How else will we pass?" His small pale face looked out of the net of shadows.

"Is that what you think then?" said Malcolm, casually. "Perhaps you're right. You may be right."

"Of course I'm right. Why, I knew a chap and he wrote down all the answers to all the questions for the last ten years. I mean the same question is bound to turn up now and again."

"Yes, I'm sure you're right. The same things do turn up. That's sure. Tell me," said Malcolm, "if you won a bursary would you like to have your name in the paper?"

"What would I want to have my name in the paper for? That's no use to anybody. I'm not interested in that. I want to be able to have a career."

"What are you going to do?"

"I think I'd like to be a doctor. Of course history won't be any use to me as a doctor but I want to take it because it's one of my best subjects."

"Good for you," said Malcolm. "I mean you'll make a lot of money as a doctor and it's a useful career."

James eyes flashed gratefully. He was humble again and pleased and obliged to Malcolm. He quite liked Malcolm really though he sometimes thought that he was a bit of a romantic and a favourite with the teachers. Like that woman, their registered teacher when they were in the first year, who had found out that Malcolm was in the reading room and had sent down for him and had gone along to his teacher and explained everything to him and hadn't even reported Malcolm to the rector. No one would ever have done anything like that for him. But these people were so unfair. They never acted morally at all. One had to be very humble and keep out of the way of the lightning. Someday he would have power of life and death over some of them if he came back here. Why, he might even have that Gaelic teacher as a patient.

20

O N T H E O P P O S I T E side of the river from the village in which Malcolm stayed there was another village and every year, war or no war, there was a football match between the two villages which was taken very seriously indeed. On this particular Saturday a number of sailors home on leave were playing, including Donny, Dell's brother. Donny was a great favourite of Malcolm's. He was a tall heavy lad, red-faced and a great singer. In the old days one could hear him singing all over the village as early as the lark rose but as a result of the war he had become much more grim-looking and reticent.

The match was to be played on the same pitch as Malcolm and Dell had played on, but this time there would be some spectators. Nets had been got from somewhere and had been put up by willing labour, including that of Dell and Colin. The contingent from the other side of the river had hired themselves a large red bus to take them round by road, though in fact all they really had to do was to cross the river and walk through the fields. When their bus drove through the village with scarves waved out of windows and the players already wearing their green jerseys with the white collars, there was a sound of friendly booing from the assembled villagers.

About six o'clock Colin, Dell and Malcolm crossed the moor together in their football boots, jerseys and white shorts. They were all very nervous though not showing it.

Dell was saying: "They've got a good centre forward.

He's just like a tank. Portsmouth are after him," he added grimly for this centre was another player home on leave from the Navy.

Malcolm didn't say anything. He was almost sick with apprehension as he always was before any game. He felt as if he was about to vomit.

When they arrived at the pitch they took the football out and played about in front of goal. Their goalkeeper was called Snobby, a tall thin boy whose father owned a shop and who stuttered.

"H-h-harder," he shouted, jumping up and down and crouching down, his hands on his knees. He had managed to get a pair of yellow gloves from somewhere, to match his butterscotch-coloured woollen jersey. "H-h-harder," he shouted, his thin neck moving up and down like a squirrel's.

They drove balls at him from the penalty spot and he saved one or two, leaping at one point to touch a ball over the bar and landing on his back.

A few spectators shouted from the sidelines. One of them, a lame man, had attended every match that had ever been played by any village team. He thought nothing of walking seven miles to do so. He was a cobbler by trade and his greatest pleasure was to repair football boots. All other work he considered inferior and unimportant. He was standing there now leaning on his crutches and shouting: "Practise with your left foot," to Malcolm but Malcolm ignored him.

One of their best players was Trig, their right half, a small cultured player who blended into a football game so completely that one never realised that he was the star, so unobtrusive was he. He didn't speak much: his whole life was football. He didn't wear shin guards as many of the others did, and he never chewed anything during a game.

The dressing-room for the other team was the bus and when they came on to the field they were already wearing their football strips. Malcolm's team wore maroon strips, the other team green with white collars. As the opposing team from the village of Gurble came on to the field and began to practise in front of goal there was an ironical cheer directed mainly at their centre forward.

"Hey, Tank, where's your engine," shouted a small man with glasses which had been repaired with a piece of adhesive tape.

The Tank didn't appear to notice. Then after a while he turned round and bowed. The team had taken their contingent of supporters with them and they stayed up at the goal where they were practising. Malcolm noticed that his brother Colin was very quiet. He clapped him on the shoulder and said: "You just keep sending the ball up to me," but he wasn't as confident as he sounded. The defence appeared quite good with Snobby, Colin and Dell, Trig, Donny and another young boy called Tusker, but the forward line was a bit weak apart from the inside right, whose name was Trog and who was a twin of Trig. The other three—excluding Malcolm himself—were rather weak, short on speed and ideas. As Malcolm looked at the opposing team he thought that they seemed to be weightier than his own team, especially the centre forward, who really was built like a tank, with heavy thick legs and a compact body. The defence too was quite tall.

The referee in his long trousers busily ran on to the field. He whistled and the two teams ran up to the centre. He tossed. Donny called correctly and decided to play with the sun behind him, hoping that in another three-quarters of an hour it would have lost some of its dazzle.

The ball was kicked off. A movement developed on the opposing right wing and was lost in a mêlée, the right winger failing to escape with the ball. His name was Sam and he was a cook aboard one of the fishing boats. The ball was thrown in and again the Gurble team, by sheer weight, forced the ball up the centre, trying to get it through to the Tank who was lying back a little. Malcolm thought that Donny was giving him rather a lot of room to move in, especially as the right winger seemed rather fast as well. However, Malcolm realised that Donny would be rather rusty after his months in the Navy and it would take him some time to settle down. The ball came down from his own goal and swung over to the left wing. The left winger—Macmillan, a small player whose father owned the local shop—allowed it to drift over the line.

So far, the early stages of the game had been a bit of a scrimmage without either team showing any decisiveness and the spectators had begun to shout: "Come on, get a move on." "Stop dancing and get the goals." Just beside him Malcolm could see Barker, a tall friendly fellow who was considered a bit of a local wit and who was shouting out, "Hey, you there with the taxi-cab ears, miss the ball." A group had gathered round him to listen to his sallies and clapped and shouted at the slightest movement, greatly pleased when the Tank slipped and fell flat on his face as he was accelerating past Donny. Malcolm could see that Colin was having difficulty in holding the right winger, who had a trick of selling the dummy. Once he even ran past Colin without the ball at all, Colin followed him, and the right half closed in with it. From that time onwards Barker kept calling the right winger the Invisible Man. So far Malcolm himself hadn't even kicked the ball. He was beginning to think that things were going badly with the defence and was moving back up the wing to see if he could get hold of the ball for himself.

At that moment disaster struck. The right winger again eluded Colin and swung the ball back to the Tank. As Donny rushed in, rather late, the Tank unleashed a shot from about thirty yards out. Snobby didn't even see the ball. Malcolm watched him, agitatedly shouting insults at Colin and the defence in general, and throwing the ball angrily down the field as if he felt that everyone was to blame but himself. Later he could still see him leaning negligently against one of the goalposts talking to one of the spectators and obviously explaining how he couldn't have saved the shot.

The ball was centred. Malcolm saw Donny go over to Colin and speak to him quietly. He could imagine how Colin must be feeling. He also saw Dell speaking to him before the game was in motion again. This time the ball came over to the right. He moved with it, accelerating, feeling that familiar sensation of power and delight coursing through every pore of his body like a sluice opening, the ball at his right toe, keeping his eyes on it, never raising them, hearing vaguely the sound of cheering as he swung over to the right hugging the touchline, looking ahead of him low down, seeing two massive legs, like pillars in blue advancing, flicking the ball between the legs, making for the corner flag and then finding those pillars in front of him again. Strange how fast the back was though he was big. He sent the corner over but nothing came of it and the ball was in the centre of the field but this time he saw that Donny was advancing towards the Tank, cutting him off from the pass, shadowing him, his face grim and set and white, sending it down the left wing where it was lost again.

Blue Stockings was quite close to Malcolm though he didn't speak to him. Massively he chewed his chewing gum, resting his hands on his hips. Malcolm studied him, looking down at the huge muscled legs. What had he learned in that first burst? He had learned that Blue Stockings was faster than he had thought. He also had a lot of weight though he hadn't used it yet. Perhaps if Malcolm could accelerate fast enough on his inside this time instead of on his outside he might beat him. He wondered if perhaps he was equally good with both feet.

The ball had come through to Trig just behind him. With careful deliberation Trig slipped the ball past an opponent towards Malcolm. The crowd were shouting for the ball to be sent over to the right wing and Donny had decided to do this now. Most of the balls were being fed towards Malcolm, Trig and Trog. Malcolm trapped the ball and advanced on Blue Stockings as the other team rushed back to close their defence. He swung the ball over to Trog coming in fast and ran for the corner flag. Blue Stockings was caught between the two of them. He tried to block the pass but Trog had come right up to him before slipping the ball through to Malcolm. Immediately it came to him he hit it with his instep curving it up into the penalty area. It dropped into the area but the goalkeeper cleared it upfield with his gloves together. Again it swung out to the opposing right wing. The winger was on his way again, bobbing and weaving, Colin running alongside him. The winger stopped dead and as he did so Dell, who was covering up, swung the ball over to Donny who kicked it first time into touch as the Tank rushed in.

The cries from the touchline were frantic. "Come on, hurry up. Get a move on."

The ball came down into the centre again. Nobody had

been watching Trig, who had steadily been playing the opposing inside right out of the game. Cultured, smooth and nerveless—the born footballer without flash or panache—he broke through at a fast run, gained control of the ball, sidestepped an attacker, flicked it sideways to Trog who shot the ball into the net as the goalkeeper advanced, eventually diving to the wrong side.

In the ensuing pandemonium Malcolm was beginning to realise that this team wasn't as good as he had thought they were. True their right wing and their centre were dangerous but as he clapped Trog on the shoulders he suddenly thought : I was frightened because they are bigger than us. The strategy was to force them towards their left wing, their weak side. He would mention this to Donny at half time. It was just like playing draughts, watching out for the weak side. He felt himself part of this village team as the game progressed. He liked playing with Trig behind him. Trig had been with him in the same class at school and so had his twin brother. They were both working on the fishing boats and were small, quick, natural footballers trained on that stony pitch in front of the school which was bumpy and full of stones.

What a fine evening it was, too, for a game of football, not too hot, with the sun slightly warming the pitch and buttering it to a clear yellow. How white the goalposts looked. He wondered how Colin was feeling. He wasn't having a good game at all. And Donny—had he forgotten the war for the time? Before he knew where he was the whistle sounded and he ran over to the centre of the field with the rest of the team. They had no oranges so they took a swig of buttermilk each.

They all clustered round Donny, who was sitting on the ground tying his laces. The other team was clustered in another part of the field. He crouched down between Colin and Dell, arms round their shoulders. Without thinking he squeezed Colin's shoulder slightly, noticing the sweat on his hair.

"What do you think, Donny?" he said. "Their left side is weak. Can't you force them over to our right?"

Donny laughed gaily. "We've got them," he shouted, holding up his fingers and then locking them against his palm, his red face shining with a gipsy coarseness. And then suddenly he began to sing a Gaelic song, his voice reverberating over the pitch as if to prove that he wasn't at all breathless. All the spectators began to cheer as that voice rolled over the field resonant and strong, as if Donny had really forgotten the war and was back again in a world of careless youth.

Snobby sat in a corner by himself talking to a spectator. He was saying: "The backs are too slow. They're too slow. What chance did I have? He had a clear goal."

Dell inched himself over to him and then, kneeling, said, "Why don't you shut up, Snobby? Why don't you just shut up?" Snobby looked at him in a startled manner and then bent down and began ostentatiously to lace shoes which hadn't been unlaced.

Colin wasn't saying anything. He looked white and drawn. More than anything he wanted to play well. Dell whispered to him: "Keep up to him. Don't give him room to move around. That's what you have to do. We'll beat this lot any day," he said aloud, staring belligerently at Blue Stockings who was calmly picking his nose, sitting in a marmoreal pose.

"Come on then, lads," said Donny rising. "Let's get them this time." Funny how he had changed since the war. There was a new ruthlessness in his voice. Malcolm looked over to the edge of the field and there was Sheila standing on the touchline with a group of boys round her. She stared right across to him, smiling, but he didn't smile back. He felt as if he were living in another world.

Snobby was saying as they got up, "I hope they give me a better chance than they did last time. I didn't have a chance with that goal. I didn't even see it."

The whistle blew and they were off again, playing against what sun there was. Actually the glare had gone out of it, leaving the light bland and even but not dazzling.

It was their turn to kick off. The ball swung over to the right again but the movement petered out. It was sent to the centre by the opposing side. There was one stunning moment when the Tank was in the clear again, shouldering his way forward by brute force and unleashing a shot which Snobby, with two gloves together in classical style, did well to punch over the bar before falling on the ground.

"He's an exhibitionist," said Malcolm to himself, "an exhibitionist. That's all he is."

The corner was cleared and the ball came to him. He trapped it neatly, looking briefly around him. Trog was coming up alongside him again, his maroon shirt fluttering, as cool as ever, not a hair out of place. The centre forward was also up. Blue Stockings was coming up fast. Malcolm made as if to accelerate, then as Blue Stockings was all but on him, he back heeled the ball to Trog who raced for the corner flag. The pass came back absolutely true. He looked up quickly. The defence was coming up. He swung the ball back towards the oncoming Donny who swung it over the bar with a terrific shot. Now the crowd were shouting, "Come on, boys, you've got them ruined."

He heard Barker saying, "See that Tank. Someone should put chains on him." He smiled briefly, wondering if Barker himself had ever played, and began to run. He hadn't done much running, in the first half. Now he wanted to run, to be all over the field, to forage for the ball instead of waiting for it, but he controlled himself, confining his runs to the touchline. His schoolmaster had said that his main weakness was that he did too much running, but "You're no bad," he grudgingly admitted. Actually he had already scored ten goals for the school that season. He began to think of old Warhorse as they called him, an ex-sergeant major of the First World War now a PT teacher, who would actually shout in his stentorian voice, "Up school", without any shame whatsoever. Strange how when one was involved in a football game one did have these feelings of communion. One couldn't remain detached. You were dependent on your right half, on your inside right, on your centre forward for supplying the ball. Sometimes after a game he would be almost in tears. How ridiculous.

Here was the ball again. He looked at it as if at something from another world. What was he doing here? What was the ball doing here? He approached it, annexed it, saw the blue legs again approaching, said to himself, "This time. This is it." He knew absolutely instantaneously that this time there would be a goal. He knew this with an intuition that had nothing to do with logic or with weighing odds or with calculation. The familiar feeling flooded him again. He was practically opposite Sheila but he had completely forgotten about her. He was in a world of his own, open only to the cheering of the crowd and to flashes of colour on all sides of him. He had passed Blue Stockings, hardly even aware that he had done so, since his gaze was completely concentrated on the ball, and all else he saw was boots and stockings. He saw another pair of legs in front of him. He sidestepped, allowing his body to think for him, cutting off his mind almost completely. He swung the ball over to the goalmouth. He saw a flash and that was Trog again and the ball was in the net. As he clapped Trog on the back like a maniac he could almost have embraced him. Oh Lord, what a marvellous thing it was to play together like that. He could not remember having done anything himself. All he had seen were legs and boots, he knew nothing of the mazy weaving run which had led to the goal.

The ball went towards their own goalmouth. There was Colin. He was going into a sliding tackle. He was passed again, the right winger was coming up. He was crossing. The Tank was rising to the ball. He was bulleting it into the net. There was pandemonium. What on earth was happening? Why was Colin playing so badly? What was Snobby shouting now? The idiot. Why couldn't he shut up? Like a puppet there waving his hands and spitting on the ground at the side of the goalpost.

The ball was centred again. It was coming over towards him. He couldn't control it. Blue Stockings was sending it back up the pitch. There was frenzied cheering and counter-cheering on all sides now. It was like being inside a furnace. Their whole team was collapsing. He ran up to help the defence. Now Donny was bringing it up himself, his face set grimly. Colin was running up beside him. So was Dell. Donny was signalling to him without looking up from the ball. It came over to him. He breasted it down. Blue Stockings was almost on top of him. He stopped dead, holding it under his right foot. He flicked it between Blue Stockings' legs. He cut in with it faster than he had ever run in his life. He ran on, leaving the ball where it was. He dived over to the right. He felt Trig coming up behind him. The ball floated up in the air. What was happening? He looked up at the ball floating. Donny was jumping and he had missed. Please God, he said, please God, let Colin score. Let Colin score, he almost shouted. For an eternity the ball hung in the air. Colin was climbing towards it in slow motion. He headed it. It landed in the goalmouth. There was a terrific scrimmage. Dell had come rushing in and the ball was in the net.

He lay on the turf looking up at the goalposts, the sky, the legs, the players. What a game! What a fantastic game! Trig was helping him to his feet. He spoke for the first time, "We're going to win now." That was all he said and Malcolm knew that he was right. In a few minutes the game was over and they had won.

And soon they were standing by the bus saying goodbye to the other team and to the Tank, who did not appear at all disappointed and was asking Donny how married life agreed with him. Then the Tank was drinking beer and Malcolm knew that he would never be a great footballer though he had the makings of one. He knew it first because the Tank took the defeat so lightly and secondly because he was drinking the beer. And he felt sorry about this.

He felt sorry too for his brother, the more so when suddenly Sheila came rushing up to him with a theatrical gesture and threw her arms round his neck. He disengaged himself, keeping his face stern and pretending to be displeased.

He had his arm around Trig and he was saying: "We could be a great team." Trig didn't say anything. He was shaking out his jacket which had been lying by a goalpost. Dell came over.

"Have you thought about what I was saying to you?"

Malcolm knew that he was talking about the village team and didn't know what to say.

If only I could play for them, he thought. But then there were so many other things to be taken into account. And looking back on it coolly he realised that it had not been a very good game. Donny had taken too long to control the midfield. The goalkeeper was a histrionic idiot. Even now he was saying to one of the spectators: "They'll have to change their defence before I play again." He didn't even want to take his gloves off but stood about in his gear not wishing to be parted from it.

Malcolm and Dell and Colin walked home eventually across the moor, very quiet as the excitement drained out of their bodies. The sun was now setting. Colin's face was turned away from Malcolm's. One of his laces was trailing but he didn't seem to care. Suddenly he said: "That's a rough team, that lot." And Malcolm knew that he had lied to himself and he felt sad.

Leaving Dell they went together to the house in silence. Their mother watched their approach as the bus carrying the opposing team home roared along the village road.

21

It was just after the Latin class that Ronny came over to speak to him. "Can I talk to you a minute?" he asked. "There's something I wanted to say to you. Private."

"Oh? All right then."

As it happened they both had a free period at the time. Ronny must have known about it before he came over. Typical of him to have checked. They walked together outside the school as they were allowed to in good weather if they had a free period. They sat down below a classroom window, their legs sticking out towards the sun and an art class which was clustered round its teacher, a rather old woman with grey hair curled in an obsolete nineteen-twentyish way.

"What was it you wanted?" said Malcolm looking sideways at Ronny. Funny how sardonic he looked—that was the only word he could think of to describe him—sardonic. A clean-cut face like a Roman one on the back of a medal or a coin. Clean jawbone, dark eyes laughing, slow, careless, negligent expression.

"It's difficult to know where to start," said Ronny. "I suppose you don't like me."

"What was it you wanted to say?"

"It's true one does get bored now and again," said Ronny. "I suppose James told you about me. I'm sure he must have done. He tells everything. I'll tell you something. I'll be glad to get out of here." His eyes moved upward as if he were looking for a plane in the sky. "We haven't really talked much and yet I think you would be a quite interesting person. I was interested to hear of that In Memoriam article. I wish I had thought of it myself. It was original."

Malcolm remained silent, leaning against the shadowed cool stone. Further out in the sun it would be warmer.

Ronny suddenly seemed to come to a decision. "The fact is I wanted to talk to you about Janet. That girl admires you, you know." He paused. "In fact if we were living in the eighteenth century I think we might have a duel. Blunderbusses at eighteen paces." Ronny laughed a little.

"Why would we have this duel?" said Malcolm "I don't understand."

"Ah, that's because you don't understand Janet or me. She's very pretty you know. No one knows that better than you. Everyone knows that you like her, that you admire her 'from a distance', isn't that right? I think she finds you interesting because you're so aesthetic though of course she wouldn't know what the word means. She's not very brilliant, you know, but then I don't suppose you have to be very brilliant if you're Janet."

"I wish you'd get to the point."

"I will eventually but I have to explain things first. You see Janet is more like you in a way than she is like me. She comes from a village just like you. And I'm a townsboy and therefore suspected of corruption. Do you realise that when I played records for her all the records she'd ever heard were crummy old Gaelic ones, like big plates? The fact is you must understand she has old-fashioned ideas."

"All right. Carry on."

"Well in any case I'm beginning to think that she's

falling for you. Just a few hints here and there. Like for instance she keeps asking questions about you. She's become interested in you. She's curious. And of course, let's face it, I've gone out with one or two other girls, not schoolgirls, I may say, town girls. You know the type." He said this in a man-of-the-world way as if he expected Malcolm really to know. Malcolm was obscurely flattered.

"As I was saying, if we were living in the eighteenth century we would fight a duel but clearly we can't do that in the twentieth century even though there is a war. Do you realise we've been going out now for about two years? It's a long time," he added.

"It's not all that long," said Malcolm.

"Oh don't think I want to get rid of her or anything like that. In fact it was partly she who suggested it. Well shall I say the two of us really talked about it." He paused. "Have you ever read the *Red Star*?" he asked.

Malcolm said no, briefly.

"No I don't suppose you would have," said Ronny, the corner of his mouth twitching. "It's not exactly the kind of book Collins would approve of, though I'm not so sure that it's so far away from Dido and Aeneas if it comes to that. To tell you the truth I hadn't either till I met Janet. I thought it was some kind of Communist paper. Shall I tell you some of the stories they have? Well, most of them are about doctors and nurses. The doctor is usually young and often turns out to be married though the nurse doesn't know this. One story I read told of a nurse so infatuated with the doctor that she took the job as his wife's companion—the wife you understand being a cripple—and made her life a misery. She would come to her in the middle of the night and whisper the most hellish things to her and dress up and make ghost appearances. In the morning she was as fresh as a daisy and then when the woman complained the doctor and the nurse got her put in a mental home. That's one story. Of course they aren't all like that. Some are really about true love all dewy fresh. Are you following me?"

"Yes, I can appreciate that you've read the *Red Star* but I don't see the point."

"The point is very obvious. You see that's the kind of mind Janet has. Mind you, as I said before, this is nothing against her. It's just her way. She doesn't pretend to be intellectual. That's part of her charm. Well, the other night—I don't know how it started but anyway it came to the point where we decided to test each other. As I said we've been going out for two years or so. How do you know, she asked me, whether we really love each other? How do we know that our love will last? She talks like that you know. Part of this started because I turned up late one night at the flicks though it wasn't my fault. Are you following me?"

"Well," said Malcolm, "and what does the *Red Star* have to do with all this?"

Ronny moodily kicked at a pebble. "As I said, I don't know how it started but it came round to the fact that we should go out once or twice with someone else and see whether we remained true to each other afterwards. That's what it came down to. You with Janet and me with Miriam, if she will go out with me, though I imagine she's a bit strait-laced."

"Of all the cold-blooded schemes," said Malcolm. "I don't believe Janet ever agreed to this. I'm sure it must be your plan."

"Well, why don't you ask her? What do you think of it

anyway? I'm telling you she lives in the world of the *Red Star*. I'm beginning to live in it myself."

"What do I think of it?" said Malcolm. "I think it is absolutely crazy, egotistical and mad. In any case, I doubt if Miriam would have anything to do with you. She's far too religious."

Ronny smiled brightly: "Oh, I don't know about that. I think she might well come out with me. The point is you must not tell her anything about this."

Malcolm got to his feet. "Look, you do what you like but I'm having no part of this. If Janet will come out with me in her own way that's all right, but I'm not getting mixed up in any scheme of this kind."

"So you're going to run away then?" said Ronny, looking up at him quietly. "Just like Aeneas. How do you know this isn't her way of getting rid of me and putting you in my place? How do you know? You can't tell, can you?"

Malcolm sat down again. "What has Aeneas to do with this?"

"Oh, I just thought about it. The other day you were all for risk. You were against Aeneas because you called him a prig. It just struck me a minute ago when you were acting so self-righteous that that was a perfect illustration of people talking without any meaning. Mind you, I thought so at the time as well. You really think that literature has nothing to do with life."

"Who told you that?"

"Well, you act like it."

"If it gives you any satisfaction I will tell you that I don't believe that for a moment and I can't understand how you could have got hold of such an idea."

"All right then. You're unwilling to accept the challenge,

aren't you? You're unwilling to match yourself against me. That's the challenge. Can you take her away from me? What could be fairer than that? You've got your chance. You're being handed it on a plate.

"The fact is," he continued quietly, "I like Janet a lot. Naturally I can see her weaknesses. You may have thought I was being flippant but she is by far the prettiest girl in this school. She has great qualities you know. And she's strictly honourable. She insists on paying her own way though she's not rich. Why, one day my father took us out in the car and she insisted on paying for part of her dinner. God knows where she got the money from because her parents are quite poor. So you see I'm not doing it because I don't like her. It's just that we had this idea. The fact is I'm frightened of losing her. She's a bit confused at the moment and I don't believe she'll have anything to do with you after your first night at the cinema. Still, that's up to you. You're getting your chance. I guarantee if you ask her to go out with you she'll go and after that all's fair in love and war."

"Well, what can I lose?" said Malcolm to himself, and the element of the challenge was important. He didn't like the assured way in which Ronny had said that she wouldn't go out with him after the first night at the cinema. To go with her to the cinema, to speak to her for the whole night, just the two of them, to walk perhaps down the promenade after they had come out of the cinema, all these things sounded so much like gifts offered him by the gods that the very thought of them weakened him. That perfect face with the perfect lips, the clear earnest laughing eyes, the body swelling with its youthful promise, the self-confidence and pride of beauty secure in its own power, surely that could not be for him? Surely not? But here he

was being told that they were for him if he chose. And
really it fitted very well. Ronny was a gambler by nature.
It would appeal to some ironic quirk in his nature to make
this test and find that he had won after all. Perhaps he
was really growing bored with her. Even in the way he
played football this streak of the gambler was shown. Was
this riskiness a reaction against the fact that his father was
a lawyer with the best practice in town? Malcolm knew
that they were incomers and in fact he had often seen
Ronny's father, a small alert man with silver hair, who
sized you up when he saw you as if he was wondering
whether you had some business for him. Always smiling
and polite and easy in his manner. And what was that
about Dido and Aeneas? Had the idea come to him during
that lesson? Not that the comparison was really so exact.
Still, it would be typical of him that he would use this
ancient story in order to fashion something new from it,
to make it contemporary. A test. A trial. Malcolm thought
a little more. Perhaps if she did agree it wouldn't be so bad
after all. And why shouldn't she grow tired of Ronny? It
wasn't impossible. Why shouldn't she like him—Malcolm?
He wasn't ugly. He was reasonably presentable and he
wasn't stupid. But his earlier distrust flooded over him.
Why should she like him? And then again there was
Miriam. Would she really go out with Ronny? It would
be interesting to see. Wouldn't it?

Ronny was staring across at the art class. One fat pudgy
girl was looking intently at a horse in the distance and
trying to draw it. The old woman with her youthful curls
was looking over in their direction. Malcolm could have
sworn she was looking at Ronny, flirting with him in fact.
Her voice was raised so that they could hear what she was
saying.

"Now, girls, Delacroix wouldn't have drawn a horse like that. You must get at the muscles underneath."

Ronny rose and looked at Malcolm, a shadow falling across his brow and bisecting it into two halves, one of sunshine one of shade.

"Well?" he said glancing at his gold watch quickly, very like his father at that moment.

"All right," said Malcolm, "I agree."

Ronny smiled with satisfaction, looking down at his fingernails like someone who might be testing a rapier.

"I must say that I respect you for it," he said quietly. "I like people who take risks."

Malcolm let him go first and then followed at a distance.

22

THOUGH THE SUMMER remained flawless and
cloudless Malcolm's life was entering a period of turmoil.
He was preparing for his Bursary Competition and then
on the other hand there was Janet and there was the
football. Colin too was preparing to leave school and was
looking for a job: already he had bought himself a pair of
fishermen's wellingtons as he was thinking of becoming a
cook on a fishing boat. A lot of the time he was playing
football: his failure had made him difficult and moody.
Sometimes he took Malcolm away from his books to play
against him. Malcolm weighed everything up carefully and
decided that he must afford the time.

He himself lived in a kind of euphoria accompanied by
tension. Janet and he were to go to the cinema in a week's
time on the Saturday afternoon. The game between the
school and the village would be coming up soon but he
had had no time to look at the notice board, if a notice
had in fact been put up. Sometimes the games took place
in the evening, sometimes in the afternoons. He was
rather worried about Colin who was determined that he
must play in the game. He had had no time to visit Dicky,
who had been transferred from his home to the Sanatorium, which stood on a hill on the outskirts of the town, in
beautiful high wooded country. Every day he thought "I
will go" but he didn't go, for tuberculosis seemed at odds
with that beautiful summer and now that Dicky was not in
the village itself the obligation to visit him did not seem so

pressing. One day, however, he would visit him. Images of Dicky and Janet came together in his mind. On the one hand there was Dicky who was demonstrably dying and on the other there was Janet demonstrably in the first flush of her beauty. In fact she seemed to be growing prettier every day. He felt grateful to Ronny for having given him the chance to take her out. He couldn't be so bad after all, in spite of his supercilious manner. His attitude to Ronny had in fact changed completely. He spoke to him quite easily now : he was impressed by his cleverness and admired his poise. He was attracted by the cynicism of his conversation, by the calm disillusioned way in which he weighed up everything and everybody. Ronny was not sitting the Bursary Competition, he didn't think it was worth his while and he had no intention of bringing kudos to the school. Only Malcolm himself and James were sitting. The latter was working very hard, seated in the library all that long summer with piles of notebooks in front of him, all of which had meticulously written on them his name and class and, inside, masses of notes in small copperplate handwriting arranged under the most exact headings. The headings were in red ink, the information in blue.

Malcolm was thinking about Janet a lot of the time. He would speak to her oftener and they would sometimes walk from class together. She seemed gay and bright but rather tense. One day he said to her : "I wonder how Ronny is getting on with Miriam," and she half smiled and pointed. Miriam was laughing with Ronny, looking very animated. Janet said, "He'll soon have her reading the *Red Star*. You never see her with a bible now, do you? And you notice that her hair isn't in a bun as it used to be."

"One lives and learns," Malcolm thought to himself.

"Who would have thought it?" Miriam's outraged moral nature seemed to have calmed and settled as turbulent milk does. He was surprised to see Ronny leaning attentively towards her as if what she was saying to him was of great interest. "He's taken her to the flicks already," said Janet. "He took her to a horror film and told her it was of great literary importance. He's like that you know." Miriam hardly spoke to Malcolm now as if she regretted telling him so much about herself.

"What time will you be at the cinema?" he asked Janet.

Half surprised she said, "Oh I suppose any time. Quarter past two would be best."

"Yes, that will be all right," said Malcolm. If she had said quarter past two in the morning he would have answered with the same words. He had looked up the small booklet which gave advance notice of the picture. It was a Western called "Bend in the Valley". He asked her if she liked Westerns.

"Oh, I don't mind," she answered. "I like the flicks. I don't mind what it is."

Sometimes he would watch her as she in turn watched Ronny speaking to Miriam and he was consumed with jealousy. Once when she knew Ronny was watching she put her hand delicately on his arm and Ronny had looked over, grinning against the light.

Why, he might even put his arm around her in the cinema!

As he walked beside her he could smell the cool perfume which emanated from her, chaste and more desirable than a ranker one. The extraordinary thing was that Miriam's equally cool perfume made her seem virginal and sexless.

"What's it like in the hostel?" he once asked her.

She burst out laughing. "It's just dorms. The matron's

pretty niggly. We're not allowed out, not supposed to go out after half past nine. And we have study periods all the time."

"Do you do much studying?"

"Not much," she said kicking a twig on the ground with her toe.

He had dreams of being married to her. He even thought he would like to visit her house.

"Where do you stay?" he asked her.

"Oh it's the second house in the village," she answered abstractedly. "But I'm hardly ever down there except at holidays. Sometimes at weekends I stay with my aunt."

Once he had in fact taken a run on his bicycle down to her village and identified her house, with its door painted green and high storm window. He had stayed at the side of the road while the local bus passed him and with his hands resting on the handlebars had watched the house as if he were a spy. During the course of his vigil a stout, rather somnolent woman had come out of the house scattering meal to some hens which clustered round her. From the back he could see only that she had dark hair, a rather fat body, and was wearing a bluish overall. The hens were fluttering round her hopping about and pecking and she was staring woodenly into the distance. Her hands, too, were rather fat and she seemed to walk as if in a drugged sleep. When she was finished she stood looking at the hens for a moment, slowly rubbing her hands against her overall. Once she had turned and looked at him uninterestedly, knowing that he was a stranger. Her mouth was thinner than Janet's, the lips clamped together, the nose more pointed, and the throat fat and rather unwrinkled. She turned away indifferently after a while. A chill seemed to invade the afternoon as if a shadow had fallen and he had one last look at the house before he pedalled away—the door painted a cracked green and looking as if it had reared out of the earth around it. He couldn't understand why he felt so desolate staring at the soundless houses and at the bluish overall as it disappeared into the house.

In those days too his mother was continually pestering him. "You're not working as hard as you should," she would say.

He'd curse her under his breath as he drew a Horace towards him. What was dry Horace to him? He hated Horace. He was too settled in his Roman world, a connoisseur of wine and food and gardens and little houses, always nattering on about exile. He didn't like the poets of the eighteenth century either. Pope he intensely disliked. His favourites were Wordsworth and Tennyson and some of Kipling's poems which went with a terrific swing.

Sheila too was becoming rather troublesome to him. When he went to their house she would be in the room most of the time. He would play a game of draughts with her father and she would stand behind him watching. He won most of the games because her father wasn't really Dicky's standard. He was a big open-faced fisherman who always had a glass of beer on the table when he was playing and who would drink some, thereafter wiping his moustache, before making a move.

"Ah, some day I'll beat you," he would say humorously, not really believing it and not caring if he did or not.

Sheila wouldn't say anything but would simply stand there watching. He was often put off his game by her presence for she seemed to exude an animal warmth which troubled his mind. One of these days he would lose a game because of her. But after he had left the house she never offered to walk along the road with him. Her mother would say :

"When are you sitting the bursary?"

He was displeased at this: he wished Sheila hadn't told her about it. That summer the mother had a brother home from Africa with his wife and she would say to them, "Malcolm's going to sit a bursary you know. He's a clever boy," and the African brother would fix a bovine eye on him in silence, his slabby hands resting on his knees.

"I wish you wouldn't drink that beer," the mother would say to her husband, who would answer pacifically. "But I'm thirsty, dear. You don't know what it's like to be on the boat. I like to wash the salt out of my mouth." No ambition, that was him, no ambition at all, no drive.

And Sheila would say nothing at all but she would edge closer to him behind the chair, the clock would tick on the mantelpiece with its many small ornaments, the mother would go out to milk the cow, and all the time he could feel Sheila standing behind him while her father would study the board, half asleep as he did so, never improving. Sometimes he would actually fall asleep and begin to snore.

"Ah. I left school at fourteen," he would sometimes say. "We didn't have the chance then." Sheila would regard him with contempt.

So Malcolm would go off home in the balmy summer night, passing the dozen houses which stood between him and his home, men standing at their gates in their shirt sleeves in the twilight, the road itself glimmering in front of him and he would think : Sheila's parents must have married late. They are so much older than her. He knew that they didn't belong to the village but had moved down from the town many years before.

And he would compare Sheila with Janet. Janet was asociated in some way with a higher life, Sheila exclusively with the village. She had nothing to do with the world of books—indeed he had never seen a book in the house except once an old exercise book with the word "Geography" written on it and inside a pair of dim-looking maps showing what was called the Industrial Belt—she existed only for herself and within herself.

But Janet belonged to a different world. Though not clever herself she represented wider horizons than Sheila did. Sheila could milk a cow, stack peats, drive a horse and cart and Janet, he was sure, couldn't do any of these things. And after all they weren't important.

Sometimes at night he would watch the blue mountain which rose above the town and which he could see from the village. It was distant and ideal. Its serenity was not that of laziness but of a hard-won peace. It beckoned to the world of the spirit, tranquil and clear. But he was in those days worried also about Colin, who seemed very restless. Once Malcolm had said to him, "Isn't it your turn to go for the water today?" They brought their water to the house in buckets from the well which was about three hundred yards away but in the summer the well dried up and they had to go about a mile to the spring, carrying the two buckets to get a better balance.

"You can go yourself," said Colin abruptly, lying back on the bed.

His mother had not intervened, looking puzzled and tired. So he had gone for the water without complaint.

"You can play against yourself tonight then," he said to Colin. But Colin simply turned over and began to read his Western.

That night Colin went to the dance as usual. About

midnight, while Malcolm lay in bed staring up at the ceiling which was yellow with moonlight, he could hear Colin come in, grunting as he undressed, hanging his trousers behind a chair.

"Are you awake?" said Colin quietly.

"Yes, I'm awake."

"We'll beat you on Saturday just the same," said Colin in an affectionate tone, his voice slightly slurred as if he had been drinking. It was only much later that the significance of what Colin had said sank in.

Saturday was the day he was to go to the cinema with Janet. That night he had a troubled dream. He saw himself sitting at the desk of a small village school, Sheila beside him, the two of them playing draughts in an endlessly somnolent afternoon.

23

"So that's what you did it for," said Malcolm.

"I don't understand what you're talking about," said Ronny leaning casually against the wall with its net of shadows.

"You knew that the match and the visit to the cinema were at the same time. You planned this whole thing. Anyone could see it. What I don't understand is why you should do it."

"Frankly, I don't see what you're talking about. The bet still holds."

"What do you mean?"

"You can take her out if you want. That hasn't changed, has it?"

"No, but the match is the same time as the cinema, isn't it? And anyway why was the information about the game put up so late?"

"I thought everyone knew about it. The dates were posted at the beginning of the session."

"That's nonsense. Who was supposed to remember all that? I'm sure it was you who held it back. Everyone knows that old Manning does what you tell him. What does he know about football?"

"I suppose that's true," said Ronny contentedly. "He doesn't really know much about football I must admit. Still, he tries his best. He feels it justifies him for being an old man and for not being in the war. But at least he's giving up his time to organise games."

There was a pause. With one eye screwed up Ronny was staring at one of his brown shoes with a startling blue gaze. Malcolm had noticed this mannerism of his when he was concentrating.

"So you say that the bet's still on."

"Of course it's still on. You don't think I'm dishonourable, do you?" Ronny laughed engagingly.

Behind the wall Malcolm could see the leaves of a tree opening and shutting, letting the sun through and then cutting it off.

"What gave you the idea for this?"

"The idea? Oh the idea came to me during the discussion we had about Dido and Aeneas. You were saying that it was wrong for Aeneas to have left her. Remember?"

Malcolm didn't know what he was going to do yet instinctively he felt that this clever person had faced him with a problem which was more than a problem. It went to the roots of his being. At the moment he could not foresee all the implications, though he was sure Ronny had worked them all out.

"Did Janet know about this?" he asked.

"Why don't you ask her?"

"Will she turn up on Saturday afternoon?"

"Of course she will. I'm telling you the bet is still on. You have the chance of taking her away from me."

"Yes, and the chance of losing my place in the football team. You know that. Manning doesn't forgive easily. Was it you who suggested all this or was it her?"

"If you asked her would you believe her answer?"

Half of Ronny's face was in the shadow of the wall, the other in sunlight, and it was while looking at this that Malcolm was struck by what he had said. It was as if a blade of ice had penetrated into his heart. She might very well lie to him. What guarantee did he have that she wouldn't? On the other hand she might be telling the truth but he wouldn't know.

He made an effort: "Could you at least tell me why you did this? Have I harmed you in some way?"

Ronny's expression was still an engagingly open one.

"Harmed me? How could you have harmed me?"

"What did you do it for then?"

"Do you expect me to tell you that?"

"That's the least you could do."

"I had no reason. It just came into my head. I just thought it would be interesting."

"Like phoning Collins?"

"If you like."

"What if I went and told Collins?"

"Oh you wouldn't do that. You're too honourable. And anyway you've no proof."

"You mean it's a kind of game, is that it?"

"It was an impulse. I don't know what you're nagging on about. I'm not going to say anything more about it. How do I know why I did it?"

Malcolm looked down at him for a long time, and then said, "You bastard," and turned away.

"What's wrong with you this afternoon, Malcolm?" said Collins. "You're not your usual self. That's the second time I've asked you a question. Another wedding, eh?"

Malcolm jerked his head up again. "I'm sorry," he said.

He was thinking. "What are you doing this for anyway? Is it all a game for you too? Is this all a façade, skin over bones? As long as we're all civilised and well-mannered then Collins will be civilised and well-mannered too. It's all a game. But what if we said to him: All this you're doing, your scansion, your irregular verbs, your wee jokes, your acting, what if we said to you: All this is a lot of damn nonsense, what would emerge then, what animal would emerge then?

And he was suddenly sick of the Latin poems, the meaningless jargon, the immature play-acting of Collins, the ridiculous swish of the authoritarian cloak.

"It won't do, you know, Malcolm, it won't do. You will simply have to get down to it. Miriam, pray continue."

Where had he got the "pray continue" from? Churchill perhaps? Wasn't that what he was supposed to say: "Pray send me a memorandum on this as soon as possible." Or so the newspapers said—if you could believe them.

He crouched miserably in his seat, cursing monotonously under his breath. There he was, supposed to be clever, and he had been played with like a child. Should he not have seen through Ronny from the beginning? Should he not have seen that he had been up to something? "I fear the Greeks even when they are bringing gifts." But all he knew about was Latin verbs: about human beings he knew nothing at all. Miriam was answering all right. She would stay within the system, dead father or no dead father.

Suppose he himself went and told Collins, "Look, it was Ronny who rang you up. He hates you. We all hate you. You think that we like you because we laugh at your jokes but can't you see that all that is false? We despise and laugh at you, and think you ridiculous." Could he bring himself to tell Collins? Well, why not? Wasn't it the truth? Wasn't the truth far better for people? He was finding out the truth. Why shouldn't others?

But he knew that he couldn't bring himself to do it, not so much to save Collins but because he just couldn't, it wasn't in his nature. He thought of his mother telling him to work harder so that he could get himself a good professional job. And he knew that Latin and English and history (the little she knew of them) were for her a means to an end. If a regulation came out that in order to get an M.A. or become a minister one would have to dissect a quota of frogs' legs or slice worms into little bits, then this wouldn't stop her urging. She would say: What's wrong with you? You haven't cut up your quota of frogs' legs tonight! Get on with it! Five hundred to be done before midnight. How can you become a minister unless you dissect your quota of frogs' legs?

James, of course, was like that. His only concern was to get to university. That was why his little envy-twisted face was bent over page after page of print. That was why he spent his hours in the large spacious library copying down long extracts about the genealogies of the Angles and the Jutes. What relationship did these abstruse and utterly uninteresting facts have to him? He wasn't even an historian. He wanted to become a doctor, be called Dr, and that was why he read all the footnotes and the bits in small print. These things didn't matter to him at all.

Sitting in his seat, Malcolm thought. Was his mistake that he had liked things for their own sake? Was that it? For instance, he liked that poem of Auden's and the section about Dido and Aeneas. They were important to him. But to people like James and the ineffably bored Ronny they weren't important at all. They were there to be used, they led to somewhere else, another destination which had nothing to do with the poem. Was that why he himself had left the village school? Was that why Mr Collins was where he was now? Did he like reading Vergil and Horace? What did they mean to him? Had he read any Latin authors since he left university? How much did he really know about the classics? Was he in the slightest bit interested, or were these authors a method of gaining his M.A.?

And even if he went and told Collins about these questions, and asked him for a possible answer, he wouldn't understand what they meant. He wouldn't even see Malcolm as a human being, he would simply begin by saying, "Ah Malcolm," but he wouldn't really be speaking to Malcolm at all, he would be speaking to an abstract student to whom he reacted as an actor might to an audience. He would address him in his usual jocular self-protective tone. No, there was no hope there.

The bell rang and he went heavily to his next class.

24

MR THIN WAS an unorthodox teacher who had a
bald head and a lot of ideas in his own subject, which was
science. It was Mr Thin who said that he hated teaching,
though he was the best teacher in the school. During the
first two terms he was forced to teach but in the summer
term he made up for this as he said by "fertilising". No
longer did he talk about magnetism and light. No longer
was he involved with experiments. What Mr Thin did in
the summer term was lecture, exactly as if his class were a
university one. There was a difference, however. No one
took any notes and anyone could ask questions. Mr Thin
had unorthodox ideas about teaching : he wanted a common room exclusively for the use of the sixth year and
their teachers. He believed that ideas were more important
than anything else in this world including Mrs Thin. But
in the first two terms he couldn't teach ideas, so he took
advantage in the summer term. The rector would have
liked to put an end to these ideas sessions but he didn't
want to lose Mr Thin, who surprisingly enough got "good
results", so he bore with them as best he could. Mr Thin
had a good conceit of himself but he had reason to, for he
was the best teacher in the school though he despised teaching. When Malcolm entered the room rather late, Mr
Thin didn't say anything : this wouldn't have been right
for after all he wanted to treat his pupils as adults. He was
saying :

"Now the thing about science is that it is impersonal.

The truths of science are true whether any human being exists or not. Even if no human being existed at all the truths of science would remain true. That was what Newton, among many others, knew." He went over to the board and drew a circle. It wasn't a very good circle. "That," he said, drawing back from the board, "is an apple." He waited for the laugh, for it didn't look like an apple. "Let us assume in any case that it is an apple. Newton saw an apple fall, or so they say. All of us have seen apples falling. Eve perhaps was one of the first to see one falling." This was the kind of outrageous thing that the rector objected to, bringing religion into science and doing it moreover in a mocking, discrediting way.

"Newton was an extraordinary man. He lived in the seventeenth century. It was a time of bad hygiene and plagues. We don't know how Newton reacted to the bad hygiene but we know how he reacted to the plague. If one were to ask who is the greatest genius the world has produced one might answer, without fear of being laughed at, 'Newton.'

"In those days mathematicians and scientists used to propound problems to each other. There was a lot of jealousy and rivalry amongst them for, though science is impersonal, scientists are human. A famous continental mathematician propounded a problem and challenged anyone to solve it. One day someone mentioned this to Newton, and he said: 'I think I've got the answer to that problem somewhere among my drawers.'" There was a roar of laughter: Miriam flushed. Mr Thin looked up innocently and proceeded:

"And it was true. He really did have the answer to this problem in his drawers. He had completely forgotten about it. A remarkable man. A truly remarkable man.

158

And the most extraordinary thing of all was that this most innocent of men outside science ended up as Master of the Mint, and, even more extraordinary than that, that he spent the best part of his life trying to work out the dates at which the prophets of the Old Testament must have lived. A complex man. A curious mixture of rationalism and superstition. But to get back to the apple. Most of us have seen an apple fall to the ground. And of course we all know about gravity. But so did Newton. But what did Newton do? What was he famous for? He didn't discover gravity, whatever that means. That is a ridiculous statement. Anyone can see apples falling to the ground, and not only apples." (Someone at the back suggested "drawers" in a whisper, but Mr Thin pretended not to hear.) "No, what Newton did was to take a leap into space and see that the same force that pulled the apple to the ground was exactly the same force as kept the Moon circling the Earth and the planets circling the Sun, except of course that the planets would fall into the Sun and the Moon into the Earth if there were no force provided by the impetus of these bodies. The greatness of Newton was to see that the laws of Earth are also the laws of Heaven. It is very simple when you see it. But you had to see it. And of course this law exists whether Newton exists or no. Newton personally has nothing to do with it: he doesn't provide this law. He only elucidates it. That is what science is about. The scientist discovers laws which are independent of himself. A scientist can be rancorous, envious, atheistic, difficult, loving, or emotional in any other way you like, but that has nothing to do with the correctness or incorrectness of the laws he discovers. These laws are not personal ones. So as a result of Newton the seventeenth century became harmonious. The Moon went round the Earth, the Earth went round the Sun. The stars were in their places. Everything was in its place. Everything was beautiful because everything was harmonious. And religion combined with science."

Mr Thin paused to put a sweet in his mouth. "I read recently an article in which a scientist said that he didn't believe that his equations were right unless they were beautiful and harmonious. Well, Newton's equations are like that. Some people argue that we put ourselves into science, that we discover what we put there ourselves, that the universe isn't rational, that we make purely human constructs. That of course is nonsense. Do they mean to say that the laws of the universe would disappear on the day that the human element was wiped out? Do they mean that there were no rational laws before man existed, in the age of the dinosaur and the pterodactyl? Do they mean that on the day man was born, he brought into the universe all its laws? This man whose knuckles as yet were touching the ground? The laws of science do not depend on us. They are there apart from us. Anything else is madness.

"We may compare science with the arts. As I have said, the laws of science are independent of us. A true scientific discovery can be repeated again and again. Can we repeat a play over and over again? Suppose you put a play on night after night with the same actors and the same audience, would the result be the same? No. It wouldn't. Why not? Because a play cannot by the nature of things be experimentally controlled. The script may remain constant but the result will always be different. And why is this? The reason is that you are dealing with human beings. Now in science the law will always turn out to be constant, no matter what scientist is making the experiment. It does not depend on him. It could be a Jew, a Nazi, a Negro, who's making the experiment. He will always get the same results if the law is a valid one. As for poetry, what law has a poet discovered? Laws, perhaps, about human beings? But there are no laws about human beings! If there were, who would have believed that the Nazis would have arisen in our century?

"No, there are no laws that have been discovered by poets or playwrights or artists. And even if one speaks of technical laws, artists very often break these. The greatest masterpieces are often created by breaking such laws. Scientific laws are subjected to the test of whether they are infinitely repeatable. I write an equation on the board and it is true for all space and all time. It is as true for Mars as it is for Earth, for Saturn as it is for the Moon. Not even a wee man in a goldfish bowl can break Newton's law.

"No, Newton showed a universe rational and harmonious. As beautiful as a clock. We cannot change the fundamental laws of the universe. The stars are in their courses and will remain so. Newton said that if he knew all the forces present in the universe he could calculate what it would be like in any number of years you care to name. The eighteenth century was based on this rational harmony. Pope's poetry emerged from it. The heroic couplet is Newtonian in essence. 'Look, look up at the stars,' said Hopkins. These are impersonal. They do not depend on us. But they give us hope. They testify to the rationality of the universe."

Dazzled, Malcolm stared into the sun.

25

A F T E R S O M E C O N S I D E R A B L E thought Malcolm decided to go and see Dell. He was told that he was fishing on the pier and he walked down through the fields which were rankly perfumed with the summer till he came to the road which led to the pier. He walked along all by himself, hearing now and again the small secretive sound made by a water rat or a vole making its way cautiously through the reeds which bordered the road, and once he did actually see a rat which looked at him with small beady bright eyes and then disappeared. The blue-keeled boats were drawn up on the shore and the waves lapped against the rocks encrusted with mussels and whelks. Sitting on a bollard on the pier was Dell, a rod in his hand inched out over the side of the stone, the line drifting in the water. Malcolm walked over the stone pier towards him, his shoes making no sound.

"Quiet, I think I've got something," said Dell, gently pulling at the rod, but whatever it was had gone and he slowly lowered the line into the water again.

There were no ships on the horizon. Behind them were the jagged rocks and the pools of briny water. Six cuddies were lying on the stone beside Dell.

"I came to ask you something," said Malcolm, squinting into the sun as Ronny did.

Dell didn't turn his head. "What is it?" he asked neutrally.

Malcolm didn't know how to begin so he said:

"What are the rules for substitutes in the game you're playing on Saturday?"

Dell turned, looking at him in an amused way, his bony jaw jutting out.

"I thought you'd know that, a scholar like you."

"No, seriously. I don't know. There are no substitutes allowed, are there?"

"No, there aren't."

"I thought as much. In that case I can't play for you."

"What are you talking about? In any case I thought you weren't going to play anyway."

"Well," said Malcolm drawing a deep breath, "the thing is I don't know whether I'll be playing till about ten minutes before the game."

"Ten minutes before the game? What are you talking about?" Dell pulled slightly at the fishing rod but there was nothing on it.

Instead of replying directly, Malcolm asked: "Have you a team for Saturday?"

"A kind of a team."

"Do you think you'll win?"

"Wait," said Dell, excitedly. "I've got something this time. It's bigger than a cuddy." He pulled up the rod slowly and as it rose in the air in a delicate arc Malcolm could see a fish bigger than a cuddy flashing silver at the tip of the line.

"I think it's a saithe," said Dell, bringing it up in a wide arc, very delicately. He laid it on the stone, took hold of the struggling fish and banged it quickly against a stone, its faintish red blood staining it and his hands. He wiped them with a rag which he took out of his pocket, leaving it lying on the pier. Then he took out a packet of Turkish cigarettes from which he extracted one. "They nearly put me off the bus for smoking one of these," he said laughingly. They were practically the only kind of cigarette obtainable and they emitted the most horrible smell.

"I was saying," said Malcolm patiently, "that I don't know whether I'll play for you or not. I'll not know till ten minutes before the game. About ten minutes or so."

"Why?" said Dell, puffing the smoke towards him and trying to produce a perfect smoke ring.

"I can't explain." And how could he explain? He didn't know himself what he was going to do yet. He might go to the cinema with Janet; on the other hand he might not At this precise moment in time he didn't know what to do. The only thing definite was that he wouldn't play for the school team. He would go to meet Janet, about a quarter past two or ten past—give or take a few minutes—and then, standing there, he would know what he would do.

"It's impossible," said Dell at last, uncorrugating his brow. "Can't be done."

"Well, I mean, if there was someone who wanted to withdraw, if I turned up, I mean, and he was willing to withdraw when he saw me coming." His words came out in stammering confusion. He himself didn't know what the situation was going to be.

"I don't understand what you're talking about," said Dell. "Not a word. Not one word." He tried for another smoke ring. "Who do you think would withdraw?"

"Look," said Malcolm beginning again, "for various reasons, which there would be no point in going into now, I don't know whether I shall be playing till ten minutes before the game. Suppose I turned up and someone withdrew. You could put me down just as a provisional reserve, couldn't you? They're not so strict in school matches as they are in adult games. If you told them for instance that you had difficulty in getting a team ready . . ."

"But we have a team ready."

"All right. But it wouldn't do any harm, would it? I mean you could put me down as a reserve, couldn't you? And then if somebody wanted to withdraw I could play. They wouldn't want you to play with ten men."

"But we don't need to play with ten men."

"Listen, Dell, listen carefully, will you listen? I've withdrawn from the school eleven. There's a reason why I don't want to play with them."

"Do you mean you've been dropped?" said Dell pointing his cigarette at him like a tycoon.

"No, I have not been dropped. Now if I make up my mind that I want to play for you in the ten minutes or so I'd have, would it be all right? I mean supposing someone would withdraw."

"You really think a lot of yourself, don't you? You think we can't win without you, don't you? Isn't that it?"

"Well, do you?"

Dell paused and then said after a while, "We'd have a better chance with you. I agree with that. But you're cutting it fine. And it would mean someone willing to withdraw, someone who would have to be told about it beforehand, and who would withdraw if you turned up."

"Well, is there someone like that?"

"The only person I can think of is Colin."

There was a silence, except for the waves lapping on the rocks. The sun dazzled the eyes if you looked into it. Malcolm found himself screwing up his one eye again and then looking down at the clobbered fish from which all light and life had faded, leaving it a dull grey.

"Colin?" he said confusedly. "But Colin plays left back and I play outside right."

"Look," said Dell, stubbing the cigarette out on the stone, "If we got you we might win. But you say you don't know whether you'll turn up. Fair enough, we'd be glad to have you. And if you don't turn up that's all right too. But the way you're talking you don't know for sure what you're going to do. I don't even know what you're talking about half the time. Anyway Colin is the weakest player in the team. No, don't say anything. He is, you know. We could pull someone else back and give you the outside right position. What do you think of that?"

"If I hadn't come by twenty-five past you could start without me, remember that," said Malcolm. "It would mean I wasn't coming. Do you understand?"

"Yes, I get it. But I wish you'd tell us why you can't say now. And I'd have to see our manager about it. Still, he'll be all right. We won't have any trouble with him."

"Dell, I don't know myself all the ins and outs of why I may not be able to come and anyway it would take too long to explain. But Colin . . . He wants to play such a lot."

"Well, that's all we can do. And the team is more important than the man. You should know that. It would be better for us to win without Colin than to lose with him. I think the others would say the same."

"All this depends on which way I make up my mind."

"You're leaving it pretty late, aren't you? Still, we can put you down as a provisional reserve anyway."

"It's not so close as all that. The football park is only two minutes away from the cinema."

"What's the cinema got to do with it?"

"Nothing. I mean it has, but it's too complicated to explain now."

He wouldn't know till the time what he would do.

"Do you want to talk to Colin yourself?" said Dell without other comment.

"I don't know."

"If you ask me, you don't know anything."

"I might talk to him. But don't you say anything to him. Nothing. If I don't turn up that's all right. You just carry on."

"Thanks very much."

"You know what I mean. I'll see Colin anyway."

"Why have you changed your mind anyway?" said Dell, casually baiting his line again. "You didn't want to play for us and now you do."

"I want to play against the school now. But I don't know what I'll do. One thing sure, I won't play *for* the school."

"You fix it up with Colin then," said Dell. "And I won't say anything. Is that all right? Are you clear of the school?"

"Yes, I went and saw old Warhorse and told him I wanted out. He said as far as he was concerned I could play for anyone I liked. I could go to hell for all he cared."

"Warhorse?"

"That's the name of one of the teachers."

"Oh. Oh I see."

There was another silence as the line floated in the water and the sea soughed against the rocks, running up in diminishing threads of white foam-like sputum.

"There isn't anyone else, I suppose, apart from Colin, and no one injured?"

"No, no one else. No one at all."

"All right then." Malcolm got up, half hesitating still as if he had something else to say. Out in the bay he could see the green island with the white sheep moving about on it. Beyond that again there was the infinite haze and through it some of the hills of the mainland could be vaguely seen. In three months' time he would be on the mainland making his way to university by train. He looked downwards to where the line drifted innocuously. He could see no fish, only seaweed, and perhaps a crab or two—if they were crabs—and then on the surface of the water the round delicate luminous circles of jellyfish opening and shutting like miniature umbrellas. He wanted to drop a stone through one of them to find out how good his aim was but knew that Dell wouldn't want him to disturb the water.

"All right then," he said, turning away. "We'll see what'll happen."

He went back past the boats, down the road again, by the rustling reeds, in the warmth of the air, his shadow following him, dark and flat against the green. Once he found a can at the verge of the road and began to kick it venomously in front of him.

26

IT WAS HALF past one on his watch. He'd been walking the town till his feet were sore. He had taken some coffee and a bun in a local café, staring out into the sunlight. He had sat there for a considerable time till the Italian owner had begun to look at him significantly, not saying anything, just looking. It was another blazing day, the sun flashing from windows and the golden weathercock above the town hall. He had stood beside the fishing boats and later had seen the bus, with the village footballers, going past the cinema up the road to the park, maroon scarves streaming out of the window. He had looked to see if he could find Colin but couldn't see him. He had explained everything to Colin, well, not quite everything. He had explained, however, why he might want to play. Colin had said he would step down. Naturally. But was there no one else? No, said Malcolm, it wasn't that Colin was considered weak, it was rather that since he was his brother it would be considered that . . . Malcolm explained to himself that the reason he wanted to play so desperately was to get his revenge on Ronny, who was the school captain, to play the school team off the park. But was that wholly true? At least he felt it was wholly true. Anyway it was only for this one game. It would never happen again. Colin would be back in the side for the next game. It wouldn't happen again. Never again.

"Why do you say 'Never again'," asked Colin.

"Nothing. No reason. I meant it was the last time I'd ask you, that's all. I didn't mean anything else."

Colin had bent down and said to him, "Do you want to try my football boots on now?"

"All right." They didn't fit.

"I'll take yours up with me," said Colin. "If you don't turn up then I'll be playing."

"That's right," said Malcolm after a while.

"I don't understand all this," said Colin. "I can see why you want to play but aren't you going to leave it a little late?"

"It doesn't matter. I can't tell you. It's private."

Colin was about to say something, looking rather puzzled. "Why the devil can't I do something about the habit I have of putting myself in other people's places?" Malcolm thought.

It would be better to study mathematics. According to old Thin you eliminate the personal. He might do that yet too. He could feel Colin thinking: "Why did they pick on me? It must be because I'm the weak link." Malcolm could feel that in his very bones, to the pit of his stomach.

"It's just this once," he said again.

He felt like a killer, so devious he was, so cheating, so deceptive. To my own brother, he thought. I'm doing this to my own brother. But after all it was only one game and he wanted his revenge on Ronny. He'd play him out of the park and beyond.

"Try on the stockings now," said Colin.

"The stockings will be all right. I don't need to try them on."

"Will you be needing shinguards if you play?" said Colin looking up at him from his kneeling position.

"No. Yes, I'd better have shinguards."

And that was that. Now he had walked himself tired and would be no use for football or anything else. Another twenty minutes and he'd go along to the cinema and find

out what he would do. Perhaps even now she was dressing
in the hostel, sitting at the mirror combing her black hair,
drawing on her stockings, pulling her dress over her head,
putting perfume on herself, powdering her face, putting on
her lipstick. He imagined her drawing on her stockings,
while the small handbag stood on her dresser in the puri-
tanical hostel room. He imagined her locking the clasp of
the handbag with her small lace handkerchief in it, looking
around for her few coins. No, neither of them was rich like
Ronny. Oh, she would come all right. He was convinced
of that. Otherwise the whole thing would be unworthy of
Ronny. It wouldn't have the correct mathematical drama.
It wouldn't be beautiful or elegant. It wouldn't be the
correct equation. It wouldn't be, as Mr Thin had said,
harmonious, like the stars of the eighteenth century, like the
heroic couplet. He found himself brushing against an old
lady in black, so frail that she almost invited a push into
the gutter. He walked on and gazed into a shop window.
It showed suits and posters saying "Worth Double".

He heard people talking behind him.

"And I said to her, you knew well that your husband
wouldn't like it, him being away in the war an' all."

He could see some people already going up to the
match, one of them smoking a pipe and saying, "The
ground should be quite dry, I would think."

He walked along till he came to the place where he ate
his dinner and went past in case he met anyone and then
walked up the brae a bit to where there was a shop showing
religious tracts in the window. A woman was hanging
clothes on a line in a tenement backcourt, her calves strong
and rather rough as she strained upwards. Beyond her he
could see the spires of the school rising into the clear sky. A
red tricycle was lying by the clothes line. He stared at the

red tricycle and the flat byzantine geometrical clothes for a long time. Had she after all agreed to come at this time for this reason and no other? Surely she must be as treacherous as Ronny. Some aristocratic instinct had prevented him from asking her right out. But she must know. Of course she must know. She must know what Ronny had been planning. Yet even if she had known, would it be as well for him to go with her even if it was the last time? It was ten to two on the yellow face of the clock above the town hall. She might already have set out from the hostel walking. Should he go and meet her? No, he would wait here just above the cinema. Already some of the spectators would be lining the pitch. Soon the game would start. A slight breeze moved his trousers. Colin would be in the dressing-room wondering what was going to happen. Only he and Dell knew.

Lord, how hot it was. Two girls went past him, their heels tap-tapping on the road. Another few minutes. No sign of her yet. He would wait here. No, he wouldn't go down to the cinema. He would wait. He would wait till quarter past two and then he'd decide. Ronny had told him that she was always early. The sun was blazing down on him, and he could feel the sweat at the back of his neck. He squinted down at the ground, at his left shoe, and was reminded that this was a mannerism of Ronny's. He felt like running. I'll go along now. I'll play in that game. I'll play him into the ground. He felt his body winged for flight. What could he not do? How he would run! With what power he would run!

And then he saw her from the brae above the cinema. She was standing outside the cinema looking up at the trailers. She must have come by some other road. He stood watching her, she unaware of him. She had a glossy black handbag slung over her arm. She absent mindedly touched her hair looking casually around her, waiting. Should she not be watching if Ronny was playing? But, of course he was playing. It was she who had decided that she would come, not Ronny.

The clock showed a few minutes past. He must hurry. What was he going to do? If he did go to the cinema with her, what would Ronny say? Would he say he had won? Had he instructed her to be early—as she was—so that the last exit would be closed? After all she was really rather early. She was standing looking up towards him, though she couldn't see him against the dazzle of the sun. He couldn't move. He was going towards her but found that he hadn't moved. All the time his mind was going round and round. "If I go, and Ronny and she spend their evenings laughing at me? Is that what it will end up as? But then she looks so desirable in her yellow dress, her bare legs. Will she report everything to Ronny? Is this all it is, an experiment on his part? Will she tell him about my gaucheness? Can I believe her? Is that what she is? Another gossip?"

She was looking at her watch and then straight into the sun as if she were expecting him to come from that direction. She looked beautiful in her summer frock with the handbag over her arm in the blazing fire of the sun. He walked towards her. She saw him and waited for him. As he came up to her she looked at her watch but didn't say anything. The clock above her said eleven minutes past two. He looked from her to the cinema and was overcome with a feeling of desolation. She was standing there so poised and arrogant and blazing and suddenly he knew that he wouldn't be going to the cinema after all. It was a dream. That darkness was all a dream.

The cinema doors were opening. The commissionaire

was standing there in his bright plumage and then suddenly he began to walk away from her. And then he began to run into the light towards the football ground. She shouted after him "Malcolm," but he didn't listen. He wanted to throw it all away, true or false. It was more heroic after all. He wanted to lose her. It was necessary to lose her. She shouted only once. He found himself in among a crowd of people going to the match, all jammed together. He tried to get out but the road was so narrow and there were so many people. He looked back and saw her turning away. He made as if to go back but an old man with a stick was waving it at him, "Look where you're going, can't you? No respect nowadays. No respect for the old." He bent to help him and all the time the old man was showing white spittle at his mouth. There was no one at the cinema now. He got out of the crowd and ran back. What had he been thinking of? What heroic gesture did he think he was making, like a corny Western hero? There were two or three streets she could have gone down. She might even have gone into the cinema. He ran up to the door of the cinema and saw a drowsy-looking commissionaire. "Tell me, did a young girl just go in?" The commissionaire looked down at him from a great height. "No young lady, sir." Then he stared impenetrably out to sea. Malcolm dashed away from the cinema. He saw a small car race past. In it, he could have sworn, was Ronny—and Janet. Was Ronny leaning towards her and smiling? It couldn't be true. It must be a mistake, a trick of the light. Had Ronny known exactly what he would do all the time? He rushed down another street but could see no one except two old ladies in black talking earnestly. Janet was nowhere to be seen. Perhaps it really had been she in the car. He looked at his watch, swaying.

Fifteen minutes. What should he do? Go to the match? Hunt for her?

He ran up towards the park. That must have been the two of them in the car all right. How else could she have disappeared so quickly? He pushed his way in among the people, made an opening and was soon at the gates of the park. The spectators were already crowding round the touchline. He was about to sprint for the dressing-room when he stopped. Colin would be in there waiting. He would be putting on his boots ready to go out. And soon the two teams would be coming out, the school team with Ronny at their head. Who was that at the far end of the field. Was it Janet? The dark hair shining in the sunlight. Up near that goalpost, the right-hand one. He ran towards her. He could see her, hair shining against the sun, her yellow dress. It must be her. It could have been the two of them in that car all the time. How could one not recognise that face of Ronny's, that cool, calculating face? But now perhaps if he confronted her and asked her again. That might surprise her. She wouldn't expect that. Now there was the team out, Ronny not yet to be seen. There was a loud cheer. The yellow ball was thrown forward on to the green turf. He should be out there. He had three minutes left. He sprinted towards the dressing-room, which was just behind her. But as he passed he saw that it wasn't Janet after all. It was Sheila. And as he stood gazing at her in amazement and confusion he saw the village team running out in their maroon strips and his brother third from the front, looking round at the spectators, and appearing rather nervous, his slightly freckled face white. And he thought: Well that's solved.

Sheila said: "Look who's here."

27

H E S T O O D B E S I D E her. Her hand was gently resting on the rail. She said :

"I thought you'd be playing. Why aren't you playing?"

He said nothing, thinking about why he had left Janet. Ahead of them the game was in motion. He could see Colin dancing up and down and knew that he was very nervous. "I don't care whether you have a good game or not," he thought. "I don't care about anything." Ronny arrogantly straddled the middle of the field like a god. Only he was capable of going with Janet. Only he was capable of loving her on equal terms. Only he had the power. Was that Janet over at the other goalposts or was it another reflection of Sheila?

"No," he said, "I got out of it."

"Oh," she said, "that's queer."

Their hands rested beside each other, touched. Colin cleared the ball at the same moment and then Malcolm knew that he was going to have a good game. He himself didn't look much at the game after that.

"Do you want to watch this?" he said roughly.

"Why, don't you?" said Sheila in surprise.

"No. Come on, let's go to the flicks." He sounded masterful because he didn't care whether she came or not. "You can see the team when they come off the bus. It'll last an hour and a half and anyway they won't go home at once."

"But . . ." she began.

176

"We can see the first picture anyway and then you can come back if you like."

"If that's what you want," she said. They made their way through the crowd over to the wrought iron gates, which were open. He saw the ball rising in the air and then turned away.

They walked in step down the street till they came to the cinema. It was still as hot as ever but the streets were deserted like a frontier Western town. His feet were blazing after his run to the pitch. He looked down at her black shoes and then upwards to her stockings. Their shoes clicked along together.

"Mind you," she said, "I'd have liked to watch the game." She glanced sideways at him coquettishly.

He took her arm and then she put it in his. He was very tense and fed up. They came to the cinema and he stopped at the spot where Janet had stood. Already it was like a significant monument in his life. Sheila stood beside him for a moment at the very same spot while he dug into his pocket for money for the tickets.

"Come on," he said, still half roughly, and they walked in.

"I have to go to the place," she said as he paid for their tickets.

He nodded. He waited for her in the foyer, studying the next coming attraction which showed Bob Hope and Bing Crosby wearing white hats, dancing in step, each of them with a cigarette in his mouth. They walked up the stairs together. They went up to the back seat. He let her go in first and then he followed, finding the cinema dark after the bright dazzling light outside. There were a few people in but not many. In front of him a couple were clasped together tightly.

A voice was coming from the screen. "You're a spy, Englander." Surprised, he turned his eyes to the picture. The Western must be coming on later unless they had started putting Nazis into Westerns. A Nazi, all silver, was standing looking down at a man in a chair. He had a proud arrogant bearing and bright eyes. They sat in a little constraint for a while. Then he tentatively put his arm around her. She put her hand on his shoulder, sighing. After a time they were sitting cheek to cheek.

"Englander, you tried to get the plans but you failed. You are now in our hands. You will discover what happens when you spy on the Reich."

Cheek to cheek they watched the screen, Sheila chewing steadily so that his cheek moved as she chewed.

The Englander was pulled to his feet. His tie was askew and his shirt open at the back. The silver Nazi lashed him across the face.

Malcolm's hand stole up and down her side while she crept closer. "I'll be coming in on Saturday as usual," he said, "to play draughts." The thickness of his voice seemed to give the ordinary phrase a different meaning.

The Englander rocked back on his heels from the blow. A man came up and saluted theatrically.

"Herr Oberleutnant," he said curtly.

"What ees it?" in gutturals.

"English planes reported approaching in mass, Herr Oberleutnant. They are attacking the oil installations."

The children at the front began to cheer frantically. Malcolm could hear someone saying "Ssh." The two of them were kissing now. He could feel her heart beating so strongly that it was like a hammer against his chest. He smoothed her hair back from her forehead. Her eyes were half closed as he remembered having happened once before.

She seemed to have gone all heavy in his arms. He put his arm all the way round her so that they were clasped together as tightly as they could be. His hand rested on her knee.

A roar came from the screen. Flash of bombers going in, fighters engaging each other in the sky, the sign of the swastika. Flak, gunners at their anti-aircraft guns. A face in a cockpit in a black helmet. A parachute opening like a flower or an umbrella, drifting, twisting.

His hand crept above her knee. She made a small sound. Her hands caressed the hair at the back of his neck.

"It will not save you, Englander. You directed these planes here. It was you. You shall pay for it."

The silver Nazi had a gun in his hand. With the other he was scooping documents into his pocket.

They were wound so tightly in each other's arms that they could hardly breathe.

"Do you love me?" she said suddenly out of the darkness.

"Of course," he said, kissing her nose. "Of course I love you," he said thinking of something else, his hand exploring. Her hand tried to stop him weakly, then gave up the struggle.

"We'll play draughts," he said to her in that voice.

"Yes."

But all the time his mind was somewhere else.

A shot rang out from the screen. Three men had burst the door open and were firing with sten guns, crouching. "Come on, Harrison, let's get out of here. We haven't got much time."

"It's no good, fellows, we'll never get away."

"Come on."

The door opened. "Herr Oberleutnant . . ." and then the

sten gun opened fire and the silver figure with the high collar collapsed. Crescendo of cheering from the front, crescendo of music.

Their hands were clutched together under the skirt. She sat up suddenly and pushed her hair back.

"Oh really, you are a one." He turned away. He handed her a piece of chocolate, his eyes on the screen. The picture faded away and in its place the credits from the Western were rolling up.

She kept her hand on his arm. The credits rolled on. "You'll write to me when you get to university?" she said.

"Yes," knowing he wouldn't.

"I'll be expecting you to, remember." She laughed as if she had said something funny. She took out a comb and began to comb her hair.

A Western rider was standing on a hill looking down at a town. He and his horse were perfectly still, outlined against the sky. Malcolm's interest was caught by the perfect repose.

"Malcolm."

"Sh. Don't you want to watch this?"

"All right." She snuggled against him but not quite so close as before, though in a more possessive manner.

The rider was riding down the slope towards the town. He rode clattering up the one street. The people in the street looked at him as he passed, tall and proud in his black hat and black jerkin. One man was tying a horse to a railing, looked up at him, then down again. Suddenly, when the rider had passed, he scuttled along to the saloon. The rider tethered his horse to a rail and gave it an affectionate clap, took down his saddle roll and entered a small hotel. He banged a bell and a man came to him, a little old man with bowed legs and a sharp expression.

"Room please?" said the rider.

"Fer how long?"

"One night."

The hotel keeper looked up at him with the same quick glance, and then took out a book. "Sign here, feller."

The rider hesitated. It was clear that he wasn't going to write his own name. Then he took his saddle roll up to his moth-eaten room with the fly-speckled mirror and stood staring for a long time into it. He adjusted his guns in front of the glass, gave his hat a twitch and walked down the stair on high rotating heels.

"That's Gary Cooper," said Sheila.

"No it isn't," said Malcolm warmly. "Fathead."

She laughed a little in her throat.

Shot of a saloon. The rider pushed batwing doors open. People at the table looked up, including a man wearing a green eye-shade who was sitting with a hand of cards. The arrogant rider looked slowly round before ordering. How beautiful he was, thought Malcolm, how beautiful. Casual. Competent. A girl wearing red and with gold hair was staring at him through half-closed eyes, and smoking a cigarette. She walked over. "Howdy, stranger."

"Howdy," said the stranger indifferently, turning away to his drink, cupping the glass in his hand.

She put her hand on his arm. "You here long, stranger?"

"No, passing through."

"Looking for Whitey?" she looked up into his eyes.

"Mebbe. Mebbe not."

"What do you think will happen next?" said Sheila.

"They'll fight at the end. They'll have a duel at the end," he said. "On the sidewalk."

"He killed my kid brother, Whitey. Look, you keep out of this."

"You'll be killed."

"Up to him, if he's quick enough." Indifferently.

And so on till the end.

Whitey and the black stranger are standing together at the bar. The stranger says, "Drink, Whitey. One for the road." Lazy but watchful.

"One for the road, pardner," says Whitey laughing, more open, more reckless. "It was an accident. He tried to gun me down but I don't reckon you'll believe me."

"Drink up, Whitey. One for the road."

They walk out, Blackie first, to show that he isn't afraid, Whitey next, his hands hovering over his guns, that rolling walk.

The sidewalk. "I'm coming for you, Whitey, are you ready?" In the sunlight.

"Yeah, I'm ready."

They draw. Whitey falls. The girl in red—Brenda—runs out. She puts her arms round Blackie. "Oh, Lord, I'm glad you're safe." She brushes her hand against his jacket.

"I said I was passing through, Brenda."

"Yes, but you're finished now, aren't you. You can stay as long as you like."

"Sorry. Got to go. You know how it is. Someone waiting for me over there," pointing across the blue hills. He gets up on his horse, the townspeople gaping, most of them with bad teeth. He waves his hand just once as the horse clatters over the cobbles. He climbs the hill to where he was at the beginning. And then he is lost on the other side of the blue crests. Music.

The two of them walked together downstairs into the blinding sunlight, so bright it hurts their eyes.

He looks at her. She looks at him.

"Look," he says, "I've got something to do."

"Aren't you coming on the bus then? Don't you want to hear how the game went?"

"No, I made an appointment. Do you know Dicky? I said I'd go and see him. You know Dicky. He's in the sanatorium."

"Dicky? Yes, of course. Can I come with you?"

"To the sanatorium?" he said. "Aren't you afraid?"

"What for? I can go if you can."

He stopped thinking. "What about Dell?" he said. "Aren't you going with him? He might be expecting you on the bus."

"No, I'm not going with Dell."

"Don't you want to hear if they won?"

"No. Do you?"

"No. I'm finished with football."

"What ever for?"

"I'm not going to play again, that's all. And when I go to university I'm going to do maths."

"Why not?"

"Do you want to come then?"

"Yes."

"All right then. Come on. It's a good walk from here. We might see them on the way."

She put her hand in his quite casually and trustingly.

It was probable of course that when he got to university he wouldn't write to her. One never knew a thing like that. He walked on with his slightly rolling gait, in his black jacket and black hat, casting a dense shade on the road, massive and heavy, solid as a black stone.

Ahead of him appeared the rolling mesa. "Get out of my way," he said under his breath as a tall man without holsters came towards him. "Get out of my way or I'll gun you down."

His two guns hung low at his holsters.

He squeezed Sheila's hand and she looked up at him in her red gown. He frowned slightly. "Only passing through," he thought. "Twenty-four hours is all."

His black boots glittered in the light. He was the biggest man in that town. No question of it. He tightened an imaginary belt slung low and diagonally across his waist.

They walked through the woods together among the tall trees which cast dappled shadows on the ground.

"They say there are deer here sometimes," she said.

"No," he said definitely, "there are no deer."

There was a lot of greenery and moss. A rabbit or a hare suddenly jumped up in front of them and then he was gone. The tall trees made an avenue down which they walked. As he looked at her he suddenly saw that her face was green and he burst out laughing.

She was offended. "What are you laughing at?" she said.

"It's you," he said, "your face is green."

"So's yours," she answered.

The road wound to the right. In the wood there was no sound at all but that of running water which flowed underground. They passed a house, then another one, and then up at the top of the brae they saw the sanatorium. It was a big building and all the windows were wide open.

They stood at the door and pressed a bell. A nurse in white uniform came to the door. "Is it visiting time?" said Malcolm. Sheila still clutched his hand. The nurse looked at them.

"Who did you want to see?" she asked.

Malcolm was about to say "Dicky" and then he said, "Robert Morrison."

"Come with me." They walked down the cool corridors. Everything seemed to be cool and without perfume or smell of the open air even though the windows were open. Sterilised. They followed the nurse, watching her white starched uniform ahead of them. In the distance they saw two nurses wheeling a trolley piled high with clothes across the shining polished linoleum.

She stopped at a small room. It clearly wasn't the general ward.

"Fifteen minutes," said the nurse and left them. Dicky was sitting propped up in bed against the pillows, looking emaciated.

"Hello, Dicky," said Malcolm uneasily.

The window was open and he could see green leaves beyond and he could hear birds twittering. There was a tumbler on the small table beside the bed and a bunch of green grapes. Dicky seemed very lonely.

"Hullo, Malcolm." His throat seemed to be better anyway. "Long time no see."

"You remember Sheila," said Malcolm.

"Of course. Come in, the two of you."

Malcolm sat on the edge of the white bed, Sheila on the chair. She was looking around her and twisting her hands.

"Well, what's the news, Malcolm?" said Dicky out of his emaciated face.

"No news, nothing at all. There was a game of football today but I don't know the result yet." Dicky nodded as if he wasn't interested and as Malcolm continued to look round the room said:

"Looking for some poetry?"

"No, not really. I've given it up."

"You're joking," said Dicky. "How do you mean given it up?"

"I've got interested in maths."

"Have you lost interest in draughts too?"

"No, I'll play you sometime when you get out of here."

Sheila looked at him warningly when he said this.

"Fair enough," said Dicky. "It's better for me here anyway."

He coughed slightly and covered his mouth with his hand. There was a silence. Malcolm felt more and more uncomfortable and his hand slid into Sheila's who stood up and said, "Are you sure your pillows are comfortable?" Before Dicky could answer she was arranging the pillows, looking down at him tenderly.

"As a matter of fact, I doubt if we'll have another game of draughts," said Dicky suddenly.

"What did you say?"

"I said that I doubt if I'll last another three weeks."

"You don't mean that?" cheerfully.

"Oh yes I do. To tell you the truth I don't care much. I'm fed up lying about here. I get boils among other things."

"Do you have many visitors?"

"No. To be quite honest, I've never visited anyone in the sanatorium myself and I don't see any reason why they should visit me."

Malcolm looked at him for a moment. He noticed a change in him. It was as if he were looking at himself from a distance. Was it tranquillity or indifference?

"Would you like a game of draughts now?" he said.

"Of course not," said Sheila warningly. "What a lot of nonsense."

"No, I wouldn't thanks just the same. I get tired rather easily."

Malcolm could see that in spite of his pose there was terror behind the eyes. He covered his mouth whenever he coughed.

"The nurse will be coming soon," said Dicky. "There are all sorts of regulations. Tea at six in the morning, would you believe it? It's like being back in the Army again."

He looked down at his green pyjamas.

There was another long silence. Malcolm heard a bird suddenly trilling outside and listened for the variations and imagined it hidden among the dense leaves in the cooling twilight. He imagined it singing under the harmonious stars which shone even on this sanatorium. He tried to imagine the noises of the night, the coughs, the spittings, the groans, the complaints, and the nurses moving about in their starched blue and white, among the dying, and was afraid. Even under the harmonious stars. Through the door he could see into another room where a man was sitting up in bed staring ahead of him, not seeing anything. He appeared unshaven though clearly this wouldn't be allowed : it must be some darkening of the skin.

"No," said Dicky suddenly, "I can't see you giving up reading poetry."

"I'm giving it up all right." said Malcolm.

"Why?"

"Because it's false."

"What isn't false?" said Dicky, coughing again.

At that moment Malcolm looked into Sheila's eyes and thought, "You aren't false, are you? At least not for now." And he wished that he was out of there, walking with her hand through the warm green wood. Janet was somewhere else, perhaps up among the harmonious stars. And Ronny too. Among the harmonious stars.

Dicky coughed again and pulled out a large white handkerchief. Afterwards he picked out a green grape and chewed it.

"My mother brought these," he said. "She was here one day. I wish she wouldn't come. She doesn't know anything. And she makes a scene. She just doesn't know. It would be better if she didn't come. Her English isn't too good either."

He stared unseeingly into the night. The shadows of the leaves flickered on his face as if an invisible loom were plying backwards and forwards.

The nurse came to the door. "Time up," she said unsmilingly. Dicky gazed back at her, also without smiling. Malcolm stood up, trying to hide his joy that he was leaving. "I'll be coming oftener," he said, "now that I know where to come."

Sheila got up and said decisively. "I'll be coming with him. It wouldn't look good if I came on my own." Her short squat body, her coarse black hair, her largish red lips seemed to be the only real living things in the room.

The nurse stood watching the two of them, not saying anything, starched dress, very white, very stiff, very formal, unstained.

"Cheerio just now," said Malcolm. Dicky smiled and put back a grape he was going to eat. The nurse shut the door and then they were walking down the corridor again.

"Will he be all right?" Malcolm asked the nurse. She appeared not to hear the question for she didn't answer. Perhaps that was one of the forbidden questions. Finally she said after a long time, "We're not allowed to speak about our patients. You'd have to see the doctor."

As they were walking along they heard someone coughing and coughing without stopping. The sound punctuated their walk down the corridor. A radio somewhere was softly playing some Scottish dance music. Once they saw a wild face staring around it over the top of a striped pyjama jacket. They turned right, along the polished floor to the entrance hall, and walked out. Sheila's hand sought for his.

They walked away from the sanatorium. The air was slightly cooler and the grass greener. A small bird was standing in the garden with a worm trailing from its beak. They tried to find Dicky's window so that they could wave but couldn't see it. A man in a wheelchair waved at them. They entered the wood hand in hand, not speaking. Malcolm was thinking of Mr Thin's harmonious stars which would soon be rising in the sky. And from there he began to think about football and wondered for the first time which side had won. He hoped that Colin had had a good game. He thought of the warmth of the bus with all the people and wanted to be home as soon as possible. Sheila was looking at him sideways with a puzzled expression as he walked along thinking. He drew her to him and put his arm around her quite spontaneously. Perhaps he would write to her after all. They stopped against a tree and he kissed her. Below he could hear the sound of the buried water and on the edge of his mind a cough among the leaves. The harmonious stars had not yet come out. He strained against her, feeling the heat penetrating his body. Her lips were open towards the heavens which were beginning now to lose their blue and turn red. The leaves of the trees (in the place where they were standing) cut them off from the sanatorium. Everything was as yet very green.

EPILOGUE

THE TAXI DROVE up to the quay and the taxi driver got out. Then Colin and Malcolm got out. A drunk was wandering about the quay singing and waving a bottle in his right hand, spittle at his mouth. The ship itself loomed up white against the stone, some officers in white on the deck looking like waiters. The gangway was already laid down. The taxi driver led Colin to the back and Colin took the green case out of the boot. He humped it on his back and without saying anything carried it down the gangway, pretending that it wasn't heavy. Like a servant. Malcolm watched him out of a deep desolation. That moment was one of his worst, if not the worst. The taxi driver had taken out a cigarette and gone away by himself to smoke it.

Malcolm looked into the taxi where his mother was sitting very black and very frail with a sparse fur at her neck. He said, "Well then." She said: "Make sure that you write. And take aspirins if you catch a cold. And ask the landlady for a hot water bottle." He leaned down briefly and touched her dry lips with his. She almost cried but didn't. He turned away and met Colin coming back up. They shook hands like adults, Colin grinning and squeezing Malcolm's hand as if to show his strength.

Malcolm walked down the gangway and turned back once to wave. Colin had got into the taxi, into the front seat this time, and the driver was already stubbing his cigarette, stamping it carefully with his boot. Malcolm stood looking down at the green case and then turned again as the taxi accelerated and drove off, his mother waving frantically through the back window. He waved back once and then picked up his case. He descended the stairs with it, making his way to the berth which had been reserved for him, kicking aside one or two beer bottles which were lying at the foot of the stair. He wondered if James was on the boat as well and felt again the same anger and contempt. To think that James should have won the Bursary after all and he himself get nothing. Sheila's parents hadn't liked it. No doubt about it : their attitude had changed and so had Sheila's. It had been in the paper too and no way of hiding it. He made his way along the lit corridors white as milk, passing a steward on the way. It was like being in an underground prison, cell after cell on each side. He consulted the numbers on the doors and finally opened one of them. He switched on the light and saw the shining wooden dressing table with the mirror, the bed with the one grey blanket and the white sheets folded below it, the single chair at the side of the bed.

He went out to look for a lavatory and found it not far down the corridor. It was white and tiled like a palace, with lots of mirrors and liquid soap in a silver container that you tilted over into the water. He washed his hands and his face in the blazing bare light, in the marble whiteness, and dried himself with a roller towel.

Then he went back to his room, took his pyjamas out of the case, and laid them on the bed. He removed his jacket, tie, collar and trousers and shirt and laid them on the back of the chair. He put on his pyjamas and got into the bed, which was rather chilly with only the one blanket. Below him he could hear the thud of the engine.

He switched off the light and lay there in the darkness

alone for the first time in his life. Absolutely alone. From now on he was on his own. He crawled down the bed and drew aside the curtains on the porthole. Looking out he could see the water lapping against the side of the ship. It was oily and greasy and dirty, shore water. Drifting ahead of him he could see an almost swamped wooden box. So far the ship hadn't moved and he wanted her to move so that he could get out of there.

Somewhere above he thought Ronny and Janet might be moving but he wasn't sure if they would be leaving for a day or two. Ronny might not be going to the university anyway. And he himself was going to do maths. He might also study philosophy. He pulled the bedclothes up towards his chin, thinking that he felt a slight change in the hammering resonance of the engine. He moved over to the porthole again and pulled the curtains aside. Sure enough the ship was moving. He could see white waves thudding against the side of the ship and then thin green threads through the spray. But he could see nothing else except the sea high against the side of the ship which moved on absolutely majestically. He lay back on his bed again. At last he was alone. Free of everything, everyone. Ready to begin. He lay in the darkness deep in the bowels of the ship, feeling the waves thudding against the sides, imagining the bows cutting into the green water, hearing also as he dropped into sleep, high above him as if in another world, the gay laughter of the passengers from the disordered saloon, and then high above that again a piper playing "The Barren Rocks of Aden."